The Islands Tell Of It

Patty Fischer

The Islands Tell Of It
Copyright © 2021 by Patty Fischer

Supernatural Fiction / Horror / Suspense / Thriller

Library of Congress Control Number: 2021913093
ISBN-13:   Paperback: 978-1-64749-531-2
              ePub: 978-1-64749-532-9

All rights reserved. No part of this publication may be reproduced, distributed, or transmitted in any form or by any means, including photocopying, recording, or other electronic or mechanical methods, without the prior written permission of the publisher or author, except in the case of brief quotations embodied in critical reviews and certain other noncommercial uses permitted by copyright law.

Although every precaution has been taken to verify the accuracy of the information contained herein, the author and publisher assume no responsibility for any errors or omissions. No liability is assumed for damages that may result from the use of information contained within.

Printed in the United States of America

GoToPublish LLC
1-888-337-1724
www.gotopublish.com
info@gotopublish.com

Chapter One

The First Victim

I paced restlessly around my apartment not able to eat dinner or relax with a good DVD. My mind was racing as well as my pumping heart. It was seven p.m., two more hours. Looking out my kitchen window I admired the display of the late October sky, a dark indigo tinged in lavender towards the horizon. The clearness and beauty out there hit me as a gross contradiction of the rendezvous my partner Luther Charles and I were to keep at nine p.m.

Police protocol I had adhered to for the last seventeen years to be put aside. The twenty-eighth victim demanded a bold move that brought with it a voyage into something unknown.

I gathered my keys, cell phone and jacket for the neighborhood bar and grill, Unc's White Corner. Maybe a couple of shots would give me the liquid courage to see this passage into the very heart of darkness to its ultimate conclusion. I crossed the railroad tracks on 23rd street. To the left sat the small establishment with only four cars along the side parking lot.

I walked into the place where at the bar waved an older tall skinny gentleman dressed in a white starched body apron. His droopy-eyed Basset hound face smiled, making his wrinkles more pronounced.

Unc Monroe the owner of this bar and grill met my Grandpa Pete when Unc was arrested for selling marijuana in 1982. He got laid off from

Delco Remy auto manufacturing after his wife Mabel had given birth to twin boys. The only job after a year's search was an attendant at the Texaco station on 38th Street and Main. The pay was substandard, so he took up selling the illegal drug. Peter McMahan, a leading defense lawyer in Anderson was also the man who raised me after my parents died in an interstate mishap one winter night. Grandpa Pete defended Unc and was successful in getting him a reduced sentence in Pendleton Prison for five years. Both men have remained close for the last thirty-six years.

"Glenda, my beauty! What should it be?" Unc asked in a slight Irish accent.

Unc had always told Grandpa Pete, I looked more like a dark haired Super Model rather than an officer of the law. I guess, it was because of my long legs and body type where dresses would hang adequately over a frame that was kept in shape. Mabel would shake her head and lament, "What a waste of classic looks put into a detective garb of black dress pants and a drab jacket. Glenda was blessed with the hair and body of a sleek black stallion getting ready to race at The Kentucky Derby."

"I'm in the mood for something strong, some Jack on the rocks. Make it a double." I said, taking a seat in the middle of the long wooden bar. There was only one other person at the end who I acknowledged with a wave.

"Mabel's got an Irish stew on the stove, really good batch this time. Want a bowl?"

I made a face as though someone threw up on my shoes. "No, thanks, got butterflies doing a number in my stomach. The whiskey will serve me best, especially with what I am about to do in two hours."

Unc gathered a bottle from the line of available whiskeys along the lighted glass shelves behind him. "Here you go, Detective McMahan. Such a sweet cream complexion, maybe less of the Jack will be better." He mentioned.

I scowled deepening my expression of inner exasperation. "Now, Unc, don't sound like Grandpa Pete!" He shook his head and obeyed by pouring a double pour into the short glass.

I took a moderate gulp with only half of the Jack left swimming around the ice. "Have you got time to listen to something so bizarre? I guarantee you won't sleep tonight."

Unc looked around. There was the gentleman at the end of the bar, about ready to leave. There were four tables occupied. There were regulars, so he knew they would make a night of it. He said, "I'm at your service."

"It all started four months ago. There had been a lull in our case load. Detective Luther Charles, my partner became engaged. Our office of ten held a small celebration, toasting white grape juice in red Solo cups and gorging on a heavily-frosted buttercream sheet cake from Krogers." I said, then taking a large gulp from my glass to give me courage to tell this outlandish account.

Luther Charles possessed the body structure of one of the members of the NBA. His strong lanky build coupled with rich brown eyes and short cropped hair fit well with the manner in which he dressed—always worked in a suit sporting a different colored tie to match his many-colored dress shirts.

Mitch Gable, our direct superior approached Luther and I. His icy blue eyes were heavily somber. He handed Luther a paper. "Sorry to bust in on your fun. I got this Monday night from Chief Bledsoe. There's been

• •

a rather gruesome attack on a history professor from AU, Melanie Rossen. I need you and Glenda to talk to her at St. V's."

I spoke up. "If the victim is under a doctor's care, can't we wait til morning?"

Mitch's eyes glared at the both of us. His stout chest heaved up and down. Our fellow officers took the body language from our sergeant to mean, *'disappear and now'*. He continued staring and shouted, "Glenda, cancel the cavalier attitude! This bloody case has all the trappings of Jack-the-bleeding-Ripper method of operation. The hospital gave me a call for us to question the victim. Now, get going!"

Mitch Gable was Welsh from his mother's side. His accent got quite splashed with a mixture of his mother's native tongue and British exclamations when he was impatient with one of us detectives. My attitude triggered his rattling on in British intensifiers. Luther and I knew full well to shut up and do as he said.

Luther sequestered Melanie Rossen's attending doctor while I entered her room on the 5th floor of the south tower of the hospital. A short brown-skinned nurse in red scrubs was helping the patient get into a green vinyl easy chair close to the double set of windows.

"Hello, Ms. Rossen. Sgt. Mitch Gable from the Detective Division at the APD said I could speak with you." I said, easing my way into her private room.

The patient comfortable for the time being, placed her hand on the nurse's right arm. "I'll be fine, Anna."

The full-figured short nurse with the longest head of black hair I'd seen in a while whispered to me before she left us alone. She possessed a noticeable accent I was not familiar with. "Before you leave the hospital, Missy Detective, have me paged from the nurses' station."

Melanie Rossen was fairly attractive looked to be in her late thirties. She sat there with as much grace as her condition could afford her to be. "Detective, join me. I must say, I've seen better days. I'll do my best to comply with your many questions."

I lifted up the right side of my black suit jacket so she could see my badge clipped to my belt. "First, I'm Detective Glenda McMahan, my partner, Detective Luther Charles and I have been assigned to your case. Ms. Rossen, I was informed your attack occurred at Shadyside Park in the early evening hours."

"Yes, I live close by off of University Ave. I take a long run about four days a week, mostly to help me sleep. That night, I was out later than usual. I had some lesson plans to finish. I left my house around 8:00." She told me, grimacing as she put her hands over her hospital gown mid-stomach region.

"While on your run, did you feel or see anything out of the ordinary?"

"While I passed the foot bridge off of the High Street entrance, I turned to find a middle-height man with light brown hair behind me about three yards. His penetrating stare made me nervous. I came to the stretch of pavement along the lake region close to the new restaurant Bobber's Café on Alexandria Pike. I was grabbed from behind, one hand over my mouth and the other around my waist. The man dragged me down an embankment close to the water's edge. He dropped me on my back onto a pile of rocks. What I saw next defied my imagination." She stopped, shaking her head to stop from breaking down.

"Ms. Rossen, do you want to stop?"

She waved her hand at me and composed herself, taking deep breaths. "No, detective, I've got to get this out! Before he can do this to someone else and they might not survive, as I did, thank the good Lord."

"The terror of what type of thing he turned into caused me to become mute. His clothes seemed to fall away from his changing body. His strong legs kept my arms and lower body from moving around. His face, body and hands did not seem human anymore. His skin turned a grayish-green and in seconds his stringy light brown hair disappeared. As he pulled out a large egg which seemed to be a duck egg from the bunches of fallen leaves, I saw his fingernails, so sharp like that of a surgeon's knife cradling the strange looking egg, not the kind I was used to eating. His sharp nails peeled the outer layer, cradling it like a precious gem. His long red tongue shaped like a tube came down to my belly button. It went into my exposed mid-section, going deep. Strange, no pain. All I felt was pressure. His tongue whipped up, then he became angry. His eyes turned crimson red. I-I-I felt at this moment, I would not survive with what came next. His index finger, that razor sharp nail of his sliced me from my belly button to the top of my genital hairs. I screamed in deep cries of the most agonizing pain I've ever experienced. Before I passed out, I heard an eerie deep shout as he ate the peeled egg spattered with my blood, 'balut'!"

Ms. Rossen broke down. I immediately gave her some tissues from the box on the small white round table. I bent down as she had her face buried in the tissues. "Ms. Rossen, I believe it would be best if we stop now."

At that moment, Luther walked in. I turned around and motioned for him to follow me out to the corridor some ways from the bustle of the back and forth floor activities. I had not heard such a bizarre account in my fifteen years even before I came to the Detective Division on Main Street.

"Luther, this is right out of Sammy Terry's Fright Night when I was a kid. She was attacked by *The Creature From The Black Lagoon*." I said, shaking my head in utter disbelief.

"Watch it, partner! Your cynicism is showing." Luther said with a shit-eating grin. "Did you get anything that we can use?"

"Well, she gave me a word the attacker yelled out as he cut open her mid-section and served her blood over a hard-boiled duck egg. The blood-and-egg-entrée, he yelled out, 'balut'." I quipped, then spied the nurse Anna approaching us.

"Wait up, detectives. I only have a minute. Missy Melanie needs me." Anna waved excitedly. She seemed to be holding something in her left hand.

She got nose to nose with the both of us. "Detectives, I'm from the province of Capiz on the island of Panay in the Philippines. Here is my full name and my phone number. You will want to see me again."

"Why is that, Anna?" I asked, taking her card.

"Missy Detective, from the funny noises coming from your voice, you and your partner will need me to tell you of what attacked Missy Melanie." Anna said in a defiant tone. Her almond-shaped eyes held a stern look to combat my obvious unbelief and sarcasm.

In the parking lot of the Anderson Police Department on the corner of Main St. and Eleventh St., Luther and I began our investigation strategy. Under the June early evening sky we did not have much to go on. I took to gathering up information on the credibility of Melanie Rossen. Luther started with his computer research of the word 'balut' to get him going which would invariably help us begin an investigation into the very heart of darkness.

"Jesus, Mary and Joseph, all saints preserve me!" Unc cried out while giving himself the sign of the cross. Those folks seated in the tables behind us were so into their loud conversation they did not hear Unc's reaction.

• •

"What is this thing you and your partner are pursuing tonight?" Unc asked, his droopy eyes surprisingly rising up in complete terror.

I finished shots of Jack. I looked at my iPhone for the time, then pulled out a ten dollar bill for the drink and a tip. "The assailant from our recent list in the 20-30 range of victims is sometimes a vampire, sometimes a witch, and sometimes a ghoul."

Unc yelled out before I opened the door to my car. "You two get your asses back here after the deed! Tap on the back door, no way I can sleep tonight until I know you and Luther have survived."

Starting my car, I went over the word "deed", so aptly put by Unc. This deed to apprehend and see to the perpetrator's incarceration would fit into the "major-impossible" category of my backlog of experience. A speculative legend defined to law enforcement terminology as "special person of interest" does not fit in any case of investigative work, anywhere in the country or at any time in history. The very nature of what I was about to face, and bring into custody carried with it—unprecedented new ground of police work and intense downright terror.

Chapter Two

Four Months Before October

My plan to discredit Melanie Rossen failed in momentum with every lead. I started with the head of the history department at Anderson University, Floyd Mercer. I sat down in a cramped office on the second floor of Decker Hall.

The fifty-something appearance of a clumsy lanky man with a nuisance of wispy white hair on top of his head almost caused me to laugh out loud. I held my amusement back as he described in an enthusiastic tone, Ms. Rossen's capability to be a fine teacher in every way. He had sat in one of her lectures in September on the subject of the state of Germany when Adolph Hitler became chancellor in 1933. The large arena-like classroom filled to capacity grew quiet as she expounded on her vast knowledge of that pivotal moment when Hitler's power was rising.

I was directed by professor Mercer to the psychology department where a Manfred Foy was said to be Melanie's boyfriend for the last three years. I caught him at the end of his last class of the day.

He was gracious as I introduced myself. He offered me an invitation for coffee at the University Commons Building across the wooded hilly area behind the building where his department was located. I was taken immediately by his lyrical British accent and his massive wavy brown hair cupped under his chin.

"Did Mel get into the fact she had suffered a miscarriage two weeks before the attack?" He brought this important fact to my attention as we sat down with our coffees in hand.

I reacted in complete surprise, my nose scrunched up with my mouth open. "She appeared to be in so much pain. All she got out was the gruesome description of her assailant."

He gave me a face like someone who was about to throw up. "Yes, what she told me is on the scale of so bizarre it caused me to cringe in total disbelief. She went unglued with my initial reaction. Frankly, I thought her going on about his appearance, non-human kind of nonsense was from her coming out of the anesthesia."

Professor Foy huffed in a puzzled tone, then said with an off-handed candor. "I understand your leaning towards maybe she has some mental health issues. For instance when she lost the baby only four months along, she acted like it was some routine female mishap."

He pointed one of his long fingers at me. I thought what would come next was a firm rebuke. "I will give you one constant with Melanie. She is the type of person who will exhaust every measure of research to know precisely what and who attacked her. I have begun myself a read into Philippine Folklore on her urgings from her little doting nurse."

I thought to myself, *the Filipino nurse again. It would be ironic if Luther and I needed her after all'*. I asked one more question. "Could you give me the address of where her parents live?"

Bernie and Delores Rossen had been proprietors of Rossen China on the corner of Ninth and Main Street seemed like forever ago. It was currently a photography studio, aptly named Rossen Photos under the ownership of their nephew. They were living their idyllic retirement existence in a restored farmhouse off of Highway 32 close to the small town of Lapel.

Even though this was a cold call, the white-haired short-statured apple-cheeked couple were overly hospitable. I sat there in their living room evident of how proud they were of their two daughters with a large assortment of framed photographs on the wall behind where Bernie was seated.

He loudly asked me questions on gun control. I could feel his passion over the accelerated gun violence since January 2018. I cleared my throat, "Well, sir being in law enforcement. I feel having school personnel to carry concealed weapons in the schools would open a whole new can of worms, not good."

Delores Rossen brought in a silver tray of china tea cups, a plate of lemon squares and an elegant set of silver tea service. "Detective McMahan, how do you take your tea?"

I had a strong black coffee with Professor Foy, now tea with The Rossens. I would be surprised all this caffeine doesn't take my brain down the "Yellow Brick Road to The Strange and Unusual". Was I really going through some kind of bizarre mind-meld to get any kind of reasoning of this monster madness? Melanie Rossen's account played in my mind like several play-backs to an exciting yardage gain from a tight game from my favorite college football team during Thanksgiving bowl games.

I could not be rude. I told her politely, "A dollop of cream with two sugars."

The tea was surprisingly good. I took two sips and began my interview. "Has either of you seen Melanie embellish events out of proportion?"

"That type of behavior has always been the way of her younger sister. She's in films out West. Melanie has always stayed with the facts." Bernie answered first.

Delores added. "When I got to the hospital after we were informed by Manny that Melanie was walking around on her own and showering without assistance. She told me as she was eating her dinner she would tell me more after she did a careful search on this unusual type of attacker."

"Mrs. Rossen, didn't you find her account a little hard to swallow?"

"It is not for me to judge. It was something out of the strange fantasy-defined blockbusters we hear about." Delores responded, not to my satisfaction. I was expecting her to show some kind of disturbing behavior over all this.

"Are you both concerned about her going back to her place?"

"Manny told us he is staying with her until she can go back to work. Both Bernie and I will drop in on her. Her sister will be arriving from California next week." Delores informed me.

Delores walked me to the front door. I felt I didn't want to wear out my welcome. She placed her hand on my left wrist. "Detective McMahan, you are going to exhaust all your efforts to catch this horrible person. My Melanie is keeping something from us. I feel so strongly she is terrified all the time."

I wanted to give Mrs. Rossen hearty reassurances. All I could do is nod and give her a half-ass smile. After fifteen years in police work, I knew I was dealing with the unknown and that made me feel vulnerable. An inner feeling I despised.

In the car, my back pocket vibrated. I looked at the screen on my smart phone. A text from Luther: *Meet me at Community Hospital. We have another one.*

I got to the 5th floor and about to walk up to the nurses' station. I saw Luther talking to a shorter dark haired man in a long white hospital coat. Luther introduced me as I approached them. "Detective McMahan, this is Dr. Reyes who operated on Rosa Montez."

"Doctor, Luther briefly let me know there was another one related to our present case. What can you add?" I said.

"Detectives, the procedure I performed on Mrs. Montez was rather disturbing. Not something I've seen in my practice. The fetus we extracted from her womb looked to be mummified."

"What do you mean?" I asked.

"All bodily fluids and the baby's blood were sucked away. I am originally from Roxas City, a large city in the province of Capiz, in the Philippines. I had not believed this legend I had heard when I was a boy. What happened to this seven-month-old baby is the result of something I did not want to believe and have a hard time witnessing what happened to the patient." Dr. Reyes said, shaking his head with an air of confusion and terror.

Luther asked as I stood there speechless for once. "Dr. Reyes, can we look in on your patient?"

"Yes, but make it short. Her husband is with her now in Room 521." He told us, then walked off.

We knocked and slowly entered the room. Luther informed the gentleman sitting close to the bed with his head down as if he was in prayer. His wife was asleep. "Mr. Montez, forgive our intrusion. We are detectives from the Detective Division of the APD."

Mr. Montez jumped away from his wife's bedside. He waved his hands in a hysterical state. "No, I don't have to talk to you!" He came closer to Luther and I, his hands in front as if to push us out. "Our baby is gone, and the bruise on my wife's belly proves it was the Diablo Angel!" He made the sign of the cross and shouted at us in Spanish.

We got out of there quickly. In the hallway, I asked Luther. "What was that last thing he shouted?"

"Solo la policia no puede luchar contra tal mal. This meant in English—just the police cannot fight against such evil."

My initial sarcastic remark about Melanie Rossen's attacker was adding up to misrepresented. I knew I had to rethink this case. It was not *The Creature From The Black Lagoon,* but some kind of Filipino monster that had some people overwhelmingly terrified. I was feeling a twinge of Mr. Montez's apparent terror, although my investigative mind wanted to know all I could.

We went back to the division. Mitch Gable pointed at us, snapping his fingers to get into his office PDQ. We obeyed sitting down close to his scattered-papered desk.

His eyes looked like they would pop out of their sockets any minute. He demanded, "Give me something!"

"Well, sir, both attacks are related in some detail. It looks to be of the serial nature." Luther braved an answer first.

"Sarg, I've got to mention, what type of assailant we are profiling. The male seems to be some part of a legend steeped in a bizarre superstition originating from the Philippines." I added.

Mitch got up from his desk chair, began pacing the office. "Some horror show you two are telling me of. I don't want to have our city's pretty-boy mayor sniffing up my butt for answers as the attacks grow in number, or worse the attacker decides to go further with a murder!"

"Wow! You have described our predicament very well Sarg." I said, offering a compliment so his mood would not worsen. He turned around to where both of us were sitting. I took it he did not care much for my last comment. He gave me the dirtiest look. So bad, I thought he would give me a quick snap on the back of the head like my Grandpa Pete used to do.

He pointed to Luther. "Get cracking on your PC searches." He waved his index finger at my nose. "I order you to use your infamous instincts, not matter how far left field you get. And Glenda, drop your sarcasm about the first victim. I heard what you said to Luther."

"Luther, did you snitch on me?" I glared at my partner. He violently shook his head.

"It was that Filipina nurse who attended to Melanie Rossen. She called me the next day to say how rude you were to her." Mitch told me. "Now, the both of you, get out and burn the midnight oil if you have to!"

Luther and I moped out of the division to our vehicles like two kids who had lost their favorite kite. We said nothing to each other and went our separate ways.

I got home around 11:30 p.m., not tired, not wanting to watch anything on my flat screen. I scanned over my collection of novels. I looked over the shelf of all my Stephen King books, then went down to Dan Brown and Dean Koontz novels. I went up two shelves to my classic horror collection. My fingers scanned to the left—*Frankenstein* by Mary Shelley, nope, *Dr. Jeykell & Mr. Hyde* by Robert Louis Stevenson, nope. I came to Bram Stoker's *Dracula, Yeah that's the one!*

I got to the part when Mina pleaded for Count Dracula to let her drink his blood. He said to her, she did not know what she was asking him to do. He loved her too much to grant her plea. I was struck by the pathos this monstrous character was capable of and when someone who he loved dearly wanted him to grant her eternal life with him. Dracula initially did not want to make her into the monster he had become for centuries.

The phone next to my bedside rang. I jumped up from my mound of pillows almost landed on the floor. "Hello. Oh, Christ, Luther your ringing me scared me to death!"

"You must be reading from your Horror collection." He laughed.

"Yeah, Bram Stoker again, almost halfway through."

"I had to call. I've been on the computer looking up balut. This one search took me to an interesting article saying when this aswang cannot get its favorite kill, it goes to eating the gruesome delicacy of balut. This is a street food found in most islands of the Philippines where a duck or chicken egg hard boiled from an incubation time between 14 and 21 days. Get this, people are actually eating a duck fetus. It looks on the outside after peeled, dark red veins marbled among the white of the egg. Ugh!" Luther rattled on, along with sound effects of his weak stomach acting up.

"So, we have a name for this speculative bizarre thing, an aswang." I said.

"Got an idea. There is a restaurant that serves this strange and bizarre appetizer. It is located Chicago-way, in the suburb of Downers Grove. Let's take a road trip to sample and see this balut up close." Luther added.

"I'm up for that. Hey, I've been ordered to appear at Grandpa Pete's for breakfast. I won't be at the division until 9:30 a.m." I said, starting to get sleepy.

"That's cool. I'll be busy in my cubicle."

It didn't take me long to drift off into a deep sleep. My mind was quiet for now. I had no clue as the weeks ensued what kind of realm of crazy this investigation would take my partner and I.

Chapter Three

Bobber's Café

Grandpa Pete summoned me for breakfast. His invitations were deemed in delivery as commands rather than a nice thing to spend a morning meal with the man that raised me since early adolescence. Lola, his Great Dane came barreling at me as I parked my car in front of his palatial one-story Colonial Revival home on the beautiful Winding Way in the wealthy community of Edgewood.

"Lola, hey girl, I've missed you. Walk me to the door." I softly said to her, bending down to meet her strong structured face. I took my left hand to stroke her sleek reddish brown head.

A tall balding man still endued with handsome features in face and body opened the front door. I imagine I got my height from Grandpa Pete. My parents stood much shorter to him. "Glenda, you look fit. Come on in the kitchen. We are having breakfast via casual at my kitchen table. I hope you like eggs benedict."

"Only if you left out the asparagus." I said.

I sat basking in his espresso with a rich full-bodied blast of chicory mixed with the coffee. He brought over my breakfast entrée as if he was an elegant high-class waiter. "As you like it, no asparagus."

"Pete, I have a sinking suspicion, you've been talking to my sergeant." I opened our morning discussion.

"Glenda, he feels this unusual case you and Luther have been assigned to, you alone are letting your skepticism overshadow your past successes." Pete stressed, his large bushy eyebrows darting down.

"Pete, this case so far reads like some chilling horror novel. There has got to be some kind of rational explanation in the area of some kind of fright of a man, but still human. I get the inner creeps as the first victim insists on touting off some strange phenomenon and the second victim's husband shouts at us to stay away. The horror rhetoric coming at us at all sides is putting me in a most vulnerable state of mind. You know, I despise that kind of weakness." I told him.

"You know of my station in the Army where I spent eighteen months in Manila. I will not forget how the residents reacted when telling of a supernatural type of evil terrorizing those on the island of Boracay on the hottest of nights. Don't let your genius instincts get buried because of the police protocol you've been working under for the last fifteen years." Grandpa Pete said, becoming animated with his expression and his hand movements.

I ended our breakfast with a promise to keep an open mind. I was surprised of his advice being on the way-out nature. He was usually more of a bound-to-the-book type of person.

We shook hands at the front door instead of a loving family embrace. Peter McMahan was not defined by his emotional sentiment, maybe that was why I got uncomfortable with too much loving affection in my romantic relationships.

On route to my cubicle, I saw Luther's head pop out. "Hey, partner, got some Youtube videos you have to see. Get in here!"

I sat there listening to a film producer give historical accounts centuries old on this bizarre legend from the Philippines. Residents from the islands of Panay, Boracay, and even the most southern parts of Mindanao talked of this aswang—could look like a dog or a pig, a shapeshifter turning back into a woman then as the weather became hotter and the full moon came with the night, the woman would turn into a winged creature seeking its prey. There were also accounts that the woman could change her sex to a male to seek out victims.

Luther exited out of Youtube. "You know, these humans are cursed sometime in their adolescence then able to become witchlike, have visceral/vampire tendencies even tear up their victims like werewolves—all come from a belief before Christ of aswang being one of the fallen angels."

Luther exited out of YouTube to open up links where there existed artists' renditions of what this "Aswang" looked like. One image I stared at intensely. The image was a close up of the creature in full transformation—long strands of white hair with the mouth opened, bloody fangs beside the front teeth. What seemed to be of the female gender, she showed her hands with sharp claws instead of fingers. Coming up from behind her back were bat-like huge wings.

"Are these pictures for real?" I said, rolling my eyes.

"Glenda, this legend has been an oral tradition for centuries with now in modern day Catholics, 83% of most Filipinos believe this legend is real." Luther said, his dark eyes getting wider as he spoke.

"Luther, come on. How could an old legend land smack dab in 2018, crazier yet, in the Midwest!" I argued back.

"We've been given this case, so all that we have is pointing to what you viewed. I don't know about you, but I'm going to start working up a chart."

"All right, partner let me work with you here. So far we have two victims attacked on a hot summer night. If we check the calendar with what I listened to, it was also a full moon. Let's begin by making a run over to where Melanie was attacked." I suggested.

"Glenda, we went over that scene already!"

I stood up. "Won't hurt to scour over it again. I will treat you to an early dinner at Bobber's Café."

For the next hour, Luther and I carefully and methodically went over the tall grass, bits of sticks, and bunches of dried leaves in front of the embankment where the land meets the slow moving lake water. I had not seen anything yet to give Ms. Rossen's bizarre account any kind of credence. My inner psyche had been awakened to severe feelings of dread, and a pervading aura of something wicked happened here. We were about to give up when I heard crunching underneath my right loafer.

I raised my foot up very slowly. Luther cried out. "I'll be! Looks like a mess of egg shells."

I thought to bring a plastic Ziploc bag and a pair of tweezers from my pant pocket. "Here's a big one, almost enough for some kind of fingerprint."

"Leave it to you, to be prepared. Okay, girl scout, let's get up every shell, big or tiny." Luther said, laughing in between instructions.

Picking up the scattering of dingy egg shells, my instincts our sergeant bragged on me in the past kicked in. For one thing, Melanie Rossen's wording of this strange object called "Balut" was proven to exist.

There it went again, the pervading aura of something wicked grabbed my mind. I stood there, holding the ziplock bag of eggshells. I looked down at the contents, and someone or some premonition told me *hold on to your sanity, this case will take you such evil. Your mind, soul and body will experience many levels of terror.* I shook my head, hoping to think about something tangible. Luther came up with it.

Luther sighed. "Hey, I'm hungry. I'm going to take you up on your generous offer."

For 5 p.m., Bobber's Café was surprisingly crowded. The interior décor lacked any kind of alluring qualities to bring in hungry patrons. It had to be due to the good food. I looked around, and noticed a fresh paint job of blue and gray. It remained in all intents and purposes a bait and tackle shop.

The front counter shaped like a half moon was filled up. We took the only booth open along the series of windows looking out onto the quaint sequence of piers. A slim bouncy blonde with large blue eyes came to our table.

"Hi, there, is this your first time here?"

I said. "Yes, my partner here has a bottomless pit for a stomach. We have been meaning to come in. I'm sure you knew about the woman attacked real close."

"You must be the detectives on the case. I've seen nothing in the papers yet. I guess, it's better that way. I'm Kate Fisher. If you need me as a witness, I'm at your service." She offered in a girlish excited kind of way.

Luther spoke. "What did you see or hear?"

"Well, I was outside on the back part of the kitchen taking a smoke break with one of our fry cooks, Lester. We heard the most blood-curdling screams. It made me real uncomfortable. In a matter of minutes, something like a huge bird shot up and flew away. Lester who is hard of hearing couldn't get over the noise. He said it sounded like a jet overhead, hitting past the sound barrier."

She turned around as though someone was trying to get her attention. "Folks, I better take your orders. I've been at it again, flapping my gums too much."

I touched her hand, on the right where she held on to her note pad. "Katie, what do you think is the best here?"

"Lester makes the best Beer-Battered Alaskan Cod with steak fries, of course!"

"Sounds great! We'll have two of those with two coffees right away." Luther told her using his famous smile.

As soon as Katie left, two couples seated at the table of four closest to our booth came over to us. One of the older men said in an annoyed tone. "We were going to order dessert, but your detective work has made my wife upset. Our dining experience is now ruined! Why couldn't you have asked your questions in a more private manner?"

Luther volunteered to beg the pardon of the couples. His charm stemmed off some of their anger. I wanted them to disappear as soon as possible.

"You know, the man does have a point. We were insensitive." Luther said.

"Come on! I know I'm known for being a hard-nose insensitive bitch most of the time. You asked her, not me!" I blasted back.

All of a sudden I lost any defensive posture. I was averted by two men standing close to the front counter. The taller one I recognized to be Professor Foy. The other man a head shorter tugged on my inner attraction barometer which hit the highest level. His light brown hair was slicked back to reveal his gorgeous golden nut brown complexion.

"Sorry, I yelled at you. There is major gorgeous guy alert standing at the corner of the front counter! That type of eye-candy doesn't exist in this city." I said, holding out my hand.

"Can I look around? You should see your face. I haven't been privy to any indication of admiration of the male species from you in a long while." Luther said, chiding me out loud.

"You don't have to look around. They are coming this way." I said.

Before the two men sat down at their table, I suddenly felt a girlish nervousness in my stomach. Luther read by my petrified look he felt compelled to speak first when they stopped at our booth.

"Well, Glenda described you to me Professor Foy. I'm her partner, Detective Luther Charles. How's Melanie doing?"

" I'm quite proud and pleased with her progress. She putters around the house humming her favorite Billy Holiday song. Physically, she's up and running." The professor answered. He made a hand gesture towards the handsome stranger I could not stop gaping at.

"Detective McMahan and Detective Charles, this is Amado Rathbone. I say, damn impressive chap! He's been filling me in on how his recent formula of an antipsychotic drug which will revolutionize treatment for schizophrenics."

"Pleasure to meet you. Are you in the middle of an investigation?" Amado asked, his poise and way of precise elocution of words was like nothing I had come across. His amber-colored eyes stared me into speaking before I was about to swoon in front of everyone.

"Well, yes, always on for what we can investigate. We needed to fuel up. I will tell you both, if the coffee is any indication of how great the food is. You are in for a delicious dinner." I sputtered out the words, using an involuntary abundance of charm.

Both men out of earshot distance, Luther leaned in, "Your attraction is a bit on the middle-short side. If you are looking for Amado to be a dance partner, you two might look ridiculous. You're at least three inches taller."

I scrunched up my nose, glaring at him. "Please, I only thought he was a gorgeous looking guy. Can't I admire once in a while?"

In the midst of our banter, Katie arrived with our entrees. The savory aroma of our entrees hit me in the nose. I was ravenous.

The food was truly delicious. Surprisingly, we both cleaned our plates in short order. Luther waved Katie over to get our check. "Detectives, come back. We have a dreamy lemon cake on Friday nights."

Walking outside, I was hit by the stifling blast of heat in the air. "When we were routing around for information, didn't notice the humidity." I said, taking off my jacket.

We went to the forensics lab in the department's basement. Ava Mead was on hand to analyze any prints from the broken egg shells. She put each piece under the microscope after dusting them. She moved her swivel chair to her computer station for matching what she saw to the link she had pulled up on the lighted screen.

She rolled around to where we were hovering behind her back. "Go back upstairs. This could take a few hours or a few days. I will tell you one thing. These prints are not clearly human. Get out of my hair, and I will get back to you."

I found out eye-opening tidbits about Amado Rathbone. He was raised in Indianapolis, Indiana. His millionaire father, Ethan Rathbone made a lucrative living as CEO of giant drug corporation, IndyMerck. His son went on to major in chemistry as an undergrad at MIT in Cambridge, Massachusetts. Amado went on to successfully complete graduate studies in chemistry and physics at Caltech in Pasadena, California.

One surprising fact—he is now working with his sister Amora Rathbone on a formula for an antipsychotic drug at newly built medical research facility connected to IndyMerck called Saxony in Noblesville, Indiana. In her revealing close-up photo, Amora was decidedly stunning. She bore the same striking facial features as her brother, and her complexion possessed the similar light brown sheen. Only her long luxurious hair was cold black not nut brown as her brother's was.

I stayed on my computer until 10 p.m. Luther had left an hour ago, telling me Althea was threatening to throw out all his clothes onto the front lawn if he stayed in the division well into the night hours. I was getting bleary-eyed and feeling very hungry. I exited out of my computer and headed back to my apartment.

Funny my street on Ninth and Central was completely dark—no street lights on to light my way up to my humble abode. I got into my apartment, and found out immediately there was no electricity. I called my landlady, famous for staying up late.

"Hey, dear girl, a power outage close to St. Mary's Catholic Church took out the entire neighborhood of four blocks. It should be on in a couple of hours or so." She informed me.

I knew Unc's White Corner was opened until 2 a.m., so that's where I ended up for the wait. His wife Mabel was at the bar. Her round pinkish-red face wrinkled around her eyes when she smiled. "Well, Detective McMahan, haven't seen you in a while. You look tired, sweetie."

"Yeah, Mabel, I'm tired and starving. My whole block is out of electricity, some power outage. What's on the stove tonight?"

"Well, I've got ham hocks. The cornbread, second batch I took out of the oven ten minutes ago."

"That sounds like a winner. Can I have a piece of cornbread now and a Killian's Red?" I asked, using a pleading look.

"I'm on my way, my girl!"

I looked around the front room where four tables of folks who knew my grandfather waved at me. There were three men at the end of the bar I nodded politely to. This bar and grill used to be packed to the gills during the years General Motors assembly plants were going strong. Second shift workers came here after their shift to blow off steam from their fast-paced loud assembly work.

Now it was a toss-up if Unc and Mabel could keep the place opened. Retired folks that had been regulars for many a year were devoted in frequenting the place, mainly to keep sampling the delicious down-home cuisine Mabel was famous for.

I guzzled down the mug of beer, then asked for some ice water when Mabel brought my cornbread. The two other men at the end of the bar left. There was one gentleman left, drinking down an orange light brown liquid from a shot glass. I took a more examining look. It was Amado Rathbone.

Mabel came over with my order. "When did that guy get here?" I asked, pointing in such a way not to be obvious.

Mabel shrugged her shoulders and answered me. "I believe he arrived a few minutes before you did."

I waited until Mabel walked into the kitchen. I approached him by tapping him on his left shoulder. "Mr. Rathbone, I presume."

He turned and gave me an icy glance. "Oh, it's you, detective." Strange, I noticed his eyes to become darker in color than when I met him at Bobber's Café.

"Can't get enough of our quaint city?" I asked, attempting to be amusing.

He kept his head towards the bar looking down on his glass. "Detective, I apologize for my rudeness. I've much on my mind, wouldn't make adequate company for you right now."

"I'll leave you to your thoughts" I said, feeling utterly ridiculous in approaching someone who was unapproachable.

He grabbed my arm which brought me in, inches to his face. Those incredible penetrating eyes changed back to amber. He spoke very eloquently, "Detective McMahan, I find you very alluring. I do want to call on you when I'm more my charming self."

I jerked my head up and down. So shocked by his powerful magnetism, I didn't think too much about his eyes changing like a chameleon's skin. "I'd like that. You can get me at the Detective Division in the APD building."

He let go with me wasting no time to get back to my perch in the middle of the bar. Mabel was waiting for me. Her expression read to me, a mixture of curiosity and concern. "Glenda, my pretty girl, the likes of that intense young man, and you giving him your precious attention is not so good. I would tread lightly. He's carrying a wealth of darkness on those handsome shoulders."

I took her pudgy hands into mine and kissed them. "Love you, sorely I do. Stop mothering me. I'm a big girl, and an astute detective to boot."

She left shaking her head.

I ate my dinner savoring every bite. I was also savoring every word Amado said to me. Getting close to him I could smell a sweet aroma of nutmeg and vanilla. I've experienced my share of attractions since I went to the Police Academy right after graduating from high school. This was different. I felt torn, but also my bubbling excitement seemed bittersweet.

I loved the fact he was genuinely attracted to me. My detective instincts churned and rolled around in my head, fighting with my inner crush.

I went over several times in my head, what Mabel said as I finished the bowl of ham hocks. *'He's carrying a wealth of darkness on those handsome shoulders'*. I told myself to be smart only time would prove my inner cautiousness could be highly and dangerously compromised.

Still it was a shame, the only male I looked at twice in the last five years brought with him, challenging my incredible instinct. He could be connected to our case. I harbored girlish cartwheels of hoping there could be something else like a girlfriend from hell who made him act so mysteriously over his confession of attraction in my direction. Being in this job for so long, my instincts of suspicion to Amado are probably on the right track. On the hard line of sexual attraction, this mysterious brooding man got my heart racing, and my fantasy life back to resurface. As Mabel so aptly expressed, not so good.

Chapter Four
Heat Wave

Evie Fortner had a fight with her husband over her present state of pregnancy. Still light outside, she put her Nikes on and dashed out the back door. The Fortners were a couple in their forties very well established in their respective careers. Leo Fortner felt threatened with her baby now that she was in her fifth month. He voiced his disappointment that Evie was irresponsible in not terminating the pregnancy.

Their two-story red brick home was located across the road from Mounds State Park. Evie was no stranger to the mass amount of trails throughout the infamous park. She made her way to the left of the entrance walked briskly on route to the Delaware Indian burial mound. The positive energy around the mound Evie took in on many occasions.

Reaching the mound, she surmised it was getting close to 9 p.m.. She looked up at the clear indigo sky. She spoke to the shining full moon, "Hello there, you old so-and-so."

With a sudden swoop of a jolting crashing sound along with a gust of powerful wind, Evie found herself flat on her back. At first, she saw a large expanse of wings, color of charcoal—texture looked to be a close-weave netting.

In seconds, her jeans and undergarments were torn away. A man's or woman's face, she had difficulty making the sex out, turning into something grotesque and frightful. Her attacker had hideous red eyes, the distortion of monster-type features made it impossible for her to scream.

The mouth opened, large fangs for teeth looked to come down on her mid-section. Instead, a long red tongue shaped like a tube coiled out, finding its destination into her belly button. It drank greedily. The strong suction created enormous pressure with Evie still wanting to cry out but could not. The creature recoiled its tongue back into the open mouth. He or she bent down, sniffing around into her long dark auburn hair. A purring sound came forth. This usurper of a satisfied state from her inborn child was in some bizarre way giving thanks.

The winged being shot up, and disappeared into the darkness. Evie in a prostate condition managed to put on her tattered clothing. She felt incredibly weak, shaking all over. When she got on her feet, her chest hurt in such agony as though an elephant was sitting on it.

All she could think of was getting back home. She tried cleansing breaths, but her agony accelerated. The last chest pain brought her down to the ground once again. Each breath felt like it would be her last. In a matter of minutes she passed out, and breathed her last breath.

I was having my first cup of the day when the phone rang. "Glenda, you need to meet me at the burial mound at Mounds Park! This time the woman died." Luther told me, breathless.

There were four uniformed officers at the scene, along with Luther and Ray Walsh, county coroner. Ray was over the victim as I got close enough to see what kind of shape she was in. Ghastly, her eyes were open. All around her neck there was a line of small bites. My first thoughts were the bites caused by a wandering bobcat or coyote coming onto an unmoving body. Her lower abdomen was fully exposed with a huge purplish-red bruise in and around her belly button.

Ray gave Luther and I what he knew so far. "The victim has deep gashes around her neck, and her left ear was torn away. Detective, we've had reports of coyotes attacking runners at this park and Shadyside."

"Ray, I got ya' on the neck and missing ear, but the grotesque bruise on the lower abdomen doesn't look like an animal would have done that." I argued.

Luther rummaged through the victim's jeans. He pulled out a pair of keys, appearing to be a house key and two sets of car keys. "Ray, are you suggesting an autopsy to be paramount?"

"Well, yes, but you both know a family member has to give permission for that." Ray told us, getting back on his feet.

"Don't give me that look as if I asked an asinine question. You've got to realize the wounds on her neck on around her missing ear are not related to the massive hematoma around the belly area. There could be a possibility what eventually killed her happened in between the bruise and the gashes." Luther elaborated in such a deliberate way the coroner could not refute his observations.

Her body was placed in a body bag and put onto a gurney. A hysterical man dressed in a gray suit and orange tie came upon the EMT's placing the victim into an ambulance. He shouted, "Uncover her! I have to know if it's Evie!'

Two police officers grabbed him from both sides, attempting to restrain him. Luther ordered, "Officers, let him uncover her."

The man unzipped the black bag. He closed the victim's eyes. He nodded his head, then let the EMT's take her away. Luther approached the distraught gentleman. "Sir, did you know her?"

The man wiped tears from his eyes and cheeks. He spoke in a broken voice. "Yes, she was Evie Fortner, my wife. She didn't come back after a nasty fight we had. I said such awful things to her." He broke down, crying into his large square hands.

Luther and I managed to get him into Luther's black Cadillac Escalade. "Sir, what is your formal name?"

"I'm Leo Fortner. I live across the road from the entrance of this park. This place was her home away from home. She ran off as it was getting dark. I did not follow her, knowing she would eventually get home. I fell asleep on the front room sofa waiting up."

"Mr. Fortner, I apologize for this difficult next part. I have to know for expediency. To find the truth of what happened and a way to catch this assailant, we need your permission for an autopsy to be done." Luther spoke to him in a gentle sensitive way.

Sitting in the passenger side of the vehicle, Leo Fortner looked up at me while I leaned against the open SUV door. He loosened his tie. "I guess that is what has to be done. Who are you two plain-clothes officers if I need to speak with you again?"

"I'm Detective Glenda McMahan, my partner next to you is Detective Luther Charles. We probably should get you back to your house." I said, patting him gently on his right shoulder.

A few days later, the autopsy was done at Ball Memorial Hospital in Muncie, only twelve miles from Anderson. Ray Walsh was there only to observe and report. A youthful bald close-shaven Dr. Corey Lawry performed the procedure on the body of Evie Fortner.

After going through identification points about hair color, approximate weight, and other distinguishable features, he motioned for Luther and I to get closer. The coroner needed no invitation, he followed suit as the doctor was opening up the victim's abdominal area. I held it together as he revealed from taking a metal instrument to part three layers of skin and muscles. I could see a small undeveloped fetus—again in the unnerving state of mummification.

Luther ran off, retching loudly on his way to the nearby men's room. I stood there, my mind taking in like a sponge every word Dr. Lawry uttered. He looked back at Ray Walsh, "When you arrived you made the comment about a coyote doing all this damage. I don't believe in this part of the victim's body a coyote would do this. It seems to me a sucking apparatus took all of the baby's life juices, and of course, blood. The baby was five months along in a mother's womb of forty-five years."

"You're not insinuating we have a vampire in our midst?" Ray scoffed.

"Sir, I deal with what I see and know about the human anatomy." Dr. Lawry glared at the coroner, noticeable expression made me think he did not appreciate Ray's ill-timed remark.

"A better term to be used here, a human with the appetite of a visceral sucker. Which means getting nourishment from what is inside another body, entrails and what we have seen here. I'm going now to get into the circulatory system." Dr. Lawry said, moving up to the chest area.

"Look here, the both of you. The aorta is strained to the point of bursting. This left side of the heart is discolored which means she died from a massive heart attack." Dr. Lawry expressed in a strong deliberate tone.

He went on to carefully examine the opening around her left ear, and he circled her neck, talking into the microphone above. I heard Ray behind me verbally agree with Dr. Lawry this time. "Yes, as pointed out to me before the procedure these wounds do look like a wild animal like a coyote was responsible for the gashes around the victim's neck. The animal was also responsible for tearing off her left ear."

Luther got back to us as Dr. Lawry was closing her up. Ray spoke up first. "I'll let you detectives both know, my report will only include a miscarriage leading to the heart attack along with the animal gashes. I will also put in my report that it was likely a coyote because of the reports from other instances in the last year."

I wanted to challenge him. Luther stepped in with his brand of diplomacy. "I understand you will do despite our findings from the last two victims. We will tell Mitch Gable our truth. You cover up what you will as city government has always done in Anderson."

We left there knowing what both of us were beginning to believe would be discounted as speculative monster-mash from our professional colleagues. Luther seemed greatly sullen after his brilliant statement to the coroner. I suggested a coffee break.

We arrived at The Toast, an established downtown diner on Main Street not too far from the Police Department building in time for lunch. The place was famous for their toasted cheeseburgers.

"Luther, do you want me to tell the waitress two toasted cheeseburger platters and two coffees?"

"I'm not hungry, just coffee." He said, looking out the window at the mid-day traffic.

I told the waitress our order, then chose my words carefully. I was afraid I was losing my partner's expertise to what was weighing down on his shoulders. "Partner, your far off ways today aren't going to do shit for this case!"

"I didn't run off because my stomach was upset. What I saw gave me the shakes because of what Althea told me last night. She's pregnant. When I saw that poor dried up fetus, it came to me how real this fantasy of a developing serial assailant could be. This thing could track down my Althea and perform the same act!"

That wasn't all Luther was fretting about. He threw at me a folded paper. "This is from Ava Mead. The prints she analyzed three times show they can be identified as animal, like a large cat."

"Well, hell! We need to keep at it and get this sick perp together. Maybe there is something to Ms. Rossen's theory of human turning into a beast of sorts. You are too damn smart not to get an edge on this thing." I said, determined not for him to entertain any more of his pity-party bullshit.

I got up and dialed Anna's phone number from the only pay phone left in Anderson. "Anna, this is Detective McMahan. My partner and I met you when we were there at the hospital to question Melanie Rossen."

So, Missy Detective, bet there are more victims and you want to know what you are looking for. All right, I'm off today. Come to my house on 1824 Sheridan Court in Grandview." Anna said in an unfriendly tone, then hung up.

I sat down at our booth. Luther was drinking his coffee. His large brown eyes looked up at me. "I've got myself together. What do we do next?"

"I called Anna. You know that nurse of the first victim. We can go on over to her house after I inhale this cheeseburger. Maybe she can give us some illumination on how to proceed." I said, my mind in full-tilt concentration to put together a way to nab this perpetrator no matter how strange the road turned out to be. Luther watched me scarf down my lunch with an expression of unbelief—on how I could eat anything after viewing the torn up body of Mrs. Fortner and her dried up dead fetus at the autopsy an hour ago.

Her small ranch-style home on the inside and outside showed she took care with keeping the place pristine as precisely as she did in caring for her patients at St. Vincent's. We were seated at her dining room table in the middle of the front room and archway opening to her kitchen.

"This is something I need to hear from you, Anna. What is an aswang?" I started the discussion.

"Aswang means in my native language, salt and garlic. Which are two things that can repel the person turned into the creature only to do such evil. Local villagers dread when a hotter than normal night comes along. Many centuries ago before Jesus Christ, there were two gods my grandmother told me about: Agooran, the good god who dominated fire, and the bad god who only knew evil, Aswang."

"In what you know. Are the victims going to be adding up, because of this heat?" Luther asked.

"Oh, yes, aswang only goes out at night for its nourishment or kill, very hot night with the full moon shining in the sky. There will be many victims until the weather changes to a storm to cool things off. Funny, here in this country, people stay home when it is cold. In my island of Panay, no one goes out when it is really hot at night." Anna said, then made the sign of the cross.

"How does this aswang develop in a human?" I asked.

"Missy Melanie told me, the attacker took out a balut, ate it over her mixed with her blood. She was not pregnant but aswang could still smell, after-odor where once a baby was to be. The balut has many meanings concerning aswang. The chicken or duck egg can repel aswang, but when the cherished fetus is denied as in the case of Miss Melanie, balut is a way the burning inside, can be calmed. As for becoming aswang, a young person eats a contaminated balut or when the gestation goes beyond the 21st week, the chick in the egg becomes alive when eaten. As the male or female comes to be an adult, live chick causes person to be able to transform into aswang, evil shapeshifter. It is a horrible curse with the person wanting all the time to be free from it." Anna sighed.

"What can someone do to keep the aswang from invading the home?" Luther asked a question, showing to me he had taken every word from Anna as a possible reality.

"Put a block of dry ice close to each entryway of the house. If someone is outside alone if they carry salt or garlic, if thrown on aswang burns them anywhere on face, the wings, and chest and legs." Anna said.

I brought up the situation in arresting and bringing this thing in. "Let's say what you've told us checks out in every detail along with what we have. This perpetrator we track down. How in the hell do we get the strength to bring it in?"

Anna got up from her chair, and paced the carpet where Luther and I were seated. "It will take more than the two of you. Round up the aswang knowing its weaknesses, then restrain it. Use the strongest of ropes, pull it up, and beat on its back until it coughs up the chick inside. The aswang will be no more, he or she you can take off to jail."

I kept silent. My mind screamed. *The more I find out, the more bizarre this thing gets. I'm slowly becoming intrigued and terrified at the same time, so I have to move on.*

Luther balked at the idea of beating it. "My God, that's gross police brutality! And, worse scenario we kill the beast!"

"Detective Charles, aswang is very strong and can get very tall, almost like giant. What Missy Melanie told me, the legs were so strong it held her arms, body and legs down. She couldn't even wiggle away." Anna stressed, getting into Luther's face.

There was silence for some minutes. What we heard from Anna rocked both of us from our very core. Luther and I had been on a few dangerous raids in the last three years with all the busts from a group of meth labs. One home located out on Highway 67 on route to Muncie, we pulled out four perps from the kitchen in the center of the house. As we were leading them out of the front door, out came a woman screaming firing away with her handgun. I turned my head and right arm holding my gun and shot her in her shoulder and leg. She fell like a stone.

I was shaken for days after that shooting. This account would take more of what I wasn't sure I had to fight it. In my position so far, not one to be scared alone walking on a dark night, or forced to use my gun on the job. This type of criminal was altogether different—defined by a mysterious mythology catching me off guard. I knew by Luther's appearance as he listened to Anna, he wasn't sure how to take the account she brought forth. We left in silence.

Without a word, we possessed the same idea by breaking away one partition to connect our office space. With more space, for the next three days we created a large wall chart. Completed from the information we had compiled so far, it seemed to be quite comprehensive.

It contained on the top, photos and detailed profiles of each of the three victims. Pertinent information of how these victims were closely related in what had been done to them and their specific injuries. When we got to Evie Fortner, we listed only one injury that related to the other two. Only difference with a star next to her photo—cause of death, massive heart attack. With large red letters there was a profile of speculative information on a visceral sucker all women had in common. We thought about using the term, "aswang" but both of us refrained from using it. This type of assailant was different enough without us being touted as crazy.

This case gave me a drive I had not experienced before. All I could think of—I would fight like hell for this case, the knowledge I lived with of more cases could drive me into a realm of an emotional tightrope, I despised. In the middle of the night, I would wake up sweating profusely. My breathing shallow, sometimes unable to get a grip. I would get out of bed. Get a short glass, pour some whiskey in it. Slowly drink it, looking out my kitchen window.

Chapter Five

Deep End Dining

Despite Luther's fiancé giving him the business of taking off on a Saturday on the auspices of an important lead, we headed for Chicago. "Boy, did she give me the stink eye and a rash of man-guilt relationship crap. Sure hope, we come away with something solid."

"I happen to have brought some leverage." I giggled, holding up a court order in case we get the silent treatment.

"How did you pull that off?"

"I finally agreed to a dinner date with the old letch Judge Newman. This lovely little document with his lovely signature was my prize." I said in a triumphant tone.

We arrived at The Singapore Sling on West Peterson Ave., in Downers Grove, twelve miles north of Chicago. A petite Asian woman dressed in a tight gold dress led us to the only table available against the east wall of the main dining room. As matter of reference, Luther showed the hostess his badge. Our identity would spread wildly among the staff.

Sure enough, there in bold black letters placed under appetizers—balut, accompanied with a Vietnamese mint sauce. "Well, partner, are you brave enough to join me?" I asked.

Luther waved me off. "Not, I'm ordering the Sling Sampler."

An Asian waiter dressed in black and white formal wear came to our table. "Welcome, can I interest you in a sweet plum wine to start off your experience with us?"

"Yes, two glasses, and we would like to see your manager as well." Luther told him, showing the waiter his badge.

In minutes, the waiter came with two wine glasses and a bottle of plum wine. "Folks, the manager will be here shortly. The bottle is on the house. While you're waiting. Can I bring you an appetizer?"

I spoke up first, "Yes, I would like the balut."

Luther ordered the Sling Sampler. He took a sip of the wine. "Wow! This is really good. Glenda, you're going to need this to chase down your dangerous appetizer."

In enough time for us to finish the first glass of wine, a handsome tall well-dressed man with the deepest brownest eyes, approached our table holding a bright red metal tray with our appetizers.

He spoke in a heavy Spanish accent. "Hello there, officers. I am Romeo Blanco, manager of The Singapore Sling. Which of you officers of the law ordered the balut?"

"I did." I said, raising my hand as though I was in school.

"So, here's your sampler, sir. You policia know me but with whom am I serving to?" Blanco spoke in a gracious manner.

Luther complied without a rebuke. "Mr. Blanco, I am Detective Luther Charles and the lady who ordered the balut is Detective Glenda McMahan. We are from Anderson, Indiana.

Blanco nodded politely, then turned his attention to me. "Madam, can I instruct you in the way to enjoy the balut?" I nodded in an affirmative way.

"Tap the pointy tip of the egg's shell, and make an opening large enough for the broth to trickle into your mouth." He instructed with his deep voice almost sounding lyrical.

I followed his every direction. The broth tasted like a mild cheddar cheese sauce. I sat there waiting for the next step with my heart beating up a storm, and sure my face was fully flushed.

Luther stared, pouring another glass of wine. His wide eyes glued to my every move. He studied the expression of my eyes and mouth. Blanco continued with the instructions, "Remove the shell, season its contents with salt, spooning some of the mint sauce onto the gestated young duck. You can nibble, but I highly suggest you eat it in two or three large spoonfuls."

I took a deep breath, making myself ready for the "deep-end experience" where the appearance would shock the bravest of consuming one of most outrageous delicacies ever to be conceived. The whites of the exposed duck egg were covered by a sprawl of blood vessels—etched all over the hard-boiled surface like tiny red tribal markings.

My first two spoonfuls went down like a slithery entry of the best of oysters-on-the-halfshell, tasting much like scrambled eggs with a pinch of zesty cayenne pepper. The last spoonful I gladly gulped down and chased with two sips of the plum wine. Luther watching this process reminded me of a young child watching a parent eat some daring serving of haggis. His expression was filled with shock and awe.

"That was not as bad as I thought it would be. It certainly is much better than when Grandpa Pete made me eat liver and onions." I looked up at Romeo smiling down on me.

I cleared my throat, ready to get what we came here for. "Mr. Blanco, I have a very imperative request of you. Do you have any individual or individuals who purchased the balut in bulk for their own personal consumption?"

I read in his wide-open eyes, he was alarmed. He slowly backed away from us. I pulled the court order out from my back pocket. "Sir, from your expression and body language, I suggest you think very carefully before running away from my request. This is a legal and binding document, my partner and I won't hesitate in using."

Blanco lowered his head, shook both his hands. He said in almost a whisper. "I will be back directly with what you've asked for."

Luther sat there staring at me. I waved my hands in front of him. "Partner, you going to be all right?"

"Wow, I must say! You were righteously fierce with him. He was on his way to bale on us. You deserve some of my delicious appetizer." Luther said, raising his eyebrows when he offered some of his food.

"No, thanks. Gotta level with you, my stomach right now is rolling in flip-flops. Not about the balut, but about the way Blanco reacted to my request."

I drank the rest of my glass of wine while Luther finished his appetizer of shrimp tempura, eggs rolls, and some Vietnamese braised noodles called Hu tiew kho.

Blanco came back. He handed me a folded up piece of white paper. I unfolded it as he stood there waiting. It was an email address—arathbone at saxonymerck dot com. My gut reaction I hid, not giving the gracious manager the pleasure in seeing me squirm.

"This person with that email is the only person I sell the balut to every month. The woman picks it up, not speaking to anyone even me. She pays a tidy sum and leaves." Blanco told us.

"What does she look like? Distinguishing characteristics, that is." Luther asked while I sat there attempting to get myself together from my inward shock.

"She has long dark hair, can't see her eyes due to her wearing dark glasses. She is medium height very shapely and always wears beautiful expensive clothes. She gets out of a black Cadillac limousine where there is a driver in the front. He gets out but stays by the outside of the car on the driver's side. I've done what you've asked. I need to see to my business. Please, detectives, the food is on the house." Blanco said, leaving our presence with a chilling farewell.

Luther winked at me as he pulled out a ten dollar bill to leave on the table. "Ante up, partner." I shook my head and pulled out a ten. Our food and drink was on the house, but at least the waiter got paid.

We drove back in silence until Luther hit I465 East heading towards I69 for Anderson. "Glenda, Blanco said it was a woman not a man."

"When I went on a search wanting to know more about Amado Rathbone, all I got was his education history. There was no photos of him. On the Saxony website, there was a stunning woman with the name of Amora Rathbone. She was identified to be his sister who is working with researchers on this new drug called Divinia. The night my block's electricity went out, went to Unc's for late night snack. I saw Amado there alone at the end of the bar." I explained.

"That doesn't sound so unusual. He probably spent the evening with Professor Foy, and wanted one for the road." Luther said.

"I went down to where he was seated, wanting to be friendly. By his sullenness and body language, he didn't want to reciprocate back. Even Mabel pointed out he was not someone I should get close to." I answered back.

Luther sighed as he drove onto the ramp to I69. "Well, it looks like we need to visit Mr. Rathbone. Did you happen to get an address on your search?"

"Yes, I did. There was a separate site when I looked up Ethan Rathbone. There was a photo of this large estate looking like one of those castles in Scotland only no drawbridge. The whole clan lives on the 1700 block of North Meridian Street in Indianapolis, where the upper crust reside." I said, using some sarcasm. Rolling around in my mind was massive mixtures of a myriad of various feelings—relief in Luther's remark of the one picking up the box of balut, a woman not a man, confusion on why Amado's image not appearing with his sister on the Saxony website, and fascination in the mystery of this wealthy Rathbone dynasty with ties to Big Pharma.

Chapter Six
Rathbone Estate

What transpired next confirmed the nurse Anna's prediction. Records temperatures of stifling heat and humidity hit up 100 degrees blanketed most of the Midwest. Our department loaded up on night patrols at both Anderson parks, and the Greenway-Cardinal trail in Muncie due to the rising count of victims.

The victim roster caused Anderson, Muncie and Indianapolis newspapers to pepper their local sections with stories of bizarre attacks targeting lone women in wooded areas in parks and mile-long trails. This advent of publishing activity led to pressure from Anderson's mayor trickling into the APD chief of police directly to Mitch Gable's office.

Luther and I were about to leave for the Rathbone residence in Indianapolis when we saw our sergeant studying our wall chart. "Sarg, any thoughts? We're getting ready to chase up another lead." I informed him.

He spoke to us with his head and eyes glued to every aspect of the contents of the chart. "We are now on fifteen, eighteen victims, only one death. You two have comprehensively detailed the when, where and why. I'm having trouble with the who or what!"

He turned around to face us. His crystal blue eyes wide in alarm, his stout chest heaving as if he was going to rip us royally in verbal terms. "Questionable to grasp. Details of a human able to shape shift into some mythical monster to satisfy some inner burning! And to say out loud, a supernatural-type baby killer! How the bloody hell do you think this office can take your findings seriously?"

"Both of us realize how utterly out-there the description of the assailant has been portrayed. For the last month, details match up. The fingerprints found on egg shells at Shadyside have been proved to be something the lab reported between human and animal!" Luther spoke up.

"I've got to alert you both. Yesterday, I got off the phone with the head of a FBI task force in the Chicago office on cases where normal predatory activity is on the unusual side. They are arriving Monday. We'll see how they react when they view this chart." Gable said, then brushed by us with his head shaking in utter disillusionment.

Our prime mode of thought for today was not to be deterred by a threat of all our efforts in jeopardy of going into the trash can. We arrived at the large stone-walled gate of the Rathbone estate around ten a.m. Luther spoke into an intercom built into the uneven gray and charcoal stones. I looked to my right and then to my left, hoping to get some glimpse of the residence.

A voice from the metal square device said, "Sir, I will inform Master Ethan of your arrival." At that, the black wrought-iron decorative gate opened. We drove up a slight rising incline of pavement with a wall of evergreens on each side of Luther's Esplanade.

The large palatial house appeared in a clearing. I caught first the sight of a tall turret on the left side of the estate. My mouth opened in awe, I said, "Well, Luther, welcome to Indy Royalty. Who would imagine such grounds and such a touch of merry old England, smack dab off one of Indianapolis's busiest streets."

The structure of the house fell under the architectural style of Tudor Revival, built in the same uneven stone work as the gate walls. The enormous home contained four sets of flat roofs and castellations all around the many rooms. The strapwork surrounding the arched ornately carved front door was a sight to behold. My left hand clanged loudly onto the brass door knocker.

A tall older silver-haired gentleman dressed in gray dress pants and a red V-necked sweater, sporting a black tie around a white shirt collar opened the door. Luther introduced us both with our unison movements of showing him our badges.

He spoke in a heavy Irish accent. "Detectives, I have informed Master Rathbone of your wish to interview him. Let me take you to him."

"Oh, sorry sir, I thought you were Mr. Rathbone." I said from behind.

"No, madam detective, I'm Wesley Thornton, the Rathbone's butler."

He led us through a succession of stately rooms. As we passed the living room there was a dark space where a stone staircase stood, looking similar to one of those from an English castle that had been built in the fourteenth century. There existed a strong cold draft from the base of a rounding staircase where the stone walls appeared quite thick

The butler noticed our reaction. He turned and said, "This staircase built by a Welsh stone mason after World War I is to The Tower where Amado and Amora share rooms on the third level."

He turned to see a dark haired woman in a dark red robe passing us to step up on the ascending the staircase. The butler only nodded at her, I gather in respect. Recognizing her, I spoke, "From your stunning photograph on your Saxony website, you resemble your great looking brother."

She stared at me, giving me a disgusting grimace. Her amber eyes turned to a noticeable dark red. She said nothing, then walked up the staircase. I wasn't put off by her stark unfriendly attitude, but inwardly I shuddered by her eyes changing colors. Wesley Thornton cajoled us to move on to the library.

"Amora is not one for people. When she's home, she only comes downstairs for food or drink. She's been a loner since she was very young. Master Ethan is waiting for you in the library." Thornton said, in his precise way of speaking.

Reaching the library, I saw Ethan Rathbone seated behind a large cherry wood desk in the Queen Anne style. He seemed in his dress and face like some distinguished lord straight out of the British royalty. His dark hair was slicked back showing gray streaks from his side profile as he was occupied on his lighted desktop computer.

"Sir, these are the detectives from Anderson you agreed to speak with." Wesley Thornton announced.

"Thank you, Wesley. Detectives, would you like coffee?" He offered as he stood showing us where to sit down.

"Yes, by all means Mr. Rathbone. We didn't get a chance for coffee at the division. Oh, By the way, I'm Detective Luther Charles, and my partner is Detective Glenda McMahan." Luther said, as he flashed his badge.

"Detectives, I'm somewhat fuzzy on why you wanted to see me." Rathbone said, sitting back down.

"Well, sir, as you know from newspaper updates, my division has been caught up in an unusual rash of savage attacks. When I saw your daughter in the hallway she looks to be of Philippine lineage as your son as well. Those professional folk in Anderson who are also Filipino have talked about their knowledge of a fierce legend going after female victims who are pregnant. We have had eighteen in total around the Anderson area." I explained.

He walked to the front of his desk close to where we were seated. "I am fully aware of Aswang. My wife Divinia came from Capiz, a province on the island of Panay."

Luther asked. "Where is she now?"

"Sadly, we are divorced many years now. Because of our daughter, Divinia could not cope with Amora's severe schizophrenia."

"Oh, that's the reason for the drug Divinia. I met your daughter before we came into the library. She seemed to look right through me, those eyes very alarming." I interjected.

Thornton brought in a tray with our coffees and a plate of triangular-shaped biscuits. He was so attentive, serving to our personal taste. "How do you both like your café?"

"I want two sugars and some cream." Luther told him.

"I want cream only. What are those puffy looking biscuits shaped like triangles?" I asked.

"Those are English tea biscuits, scones made with a marbling of cinnamon. Do you want one, detective?" He asked, smiling my way with both of our heads bobbing up and down like a couple of kids.

I bit into the warm scone, tasting so wonderful. It sure was superior in taste and texture to the balut on Saturday. When I compared the two taste tests in my head, I voiced a question.

"Mr. Rathbone, Detective Charles and I went on a road trip to a Chicago suburb where they served a Filipino delicacy quite unusual called balut. We were given a party that orders a case every month with a specific email. Do you have any idea why the email address mentioned in part with, 'arathbone'?" I explained, seeing that he began appearing quite nervous. He rubbed his hands back and forth as though they were dirty and needed to be washed.

He lowered his head, and moved back close to the arched open door. "You have to forgive me, detectives. Suddenly, I'm not feeling well. Both of you finish your coffee, then Wesley will escort you out."

I stared at Luther, and said. "Seriously. Did you see the way he just blew us off in his elitist style!"

I took the two last yummy bites of my scone, chasing it down with the rest of my coffee. Luther got up. "I guess, we better leave."

The house was so big. We were not sure which direction was the front entrance. Wesley Thornton caught up to us as we passed the stone-clad staircase. I stopped due to hearing voices high up into the cold vacuum, probably on third floor of the Tower. I motioned for Luther to stop and listen.

We both heard a sound like that of two cats in the middle of their unnerving mating ritual. Whenever I heard that type of noise in the middle of the night outside of my bedroom at Grandpa Pete's, I got up in such a state of fright. Those savage noises would always run a shudder through me at whatever age I was. As an involuntary response, both Luther and I put a grip on our guns resting in our shoulder holsters. It was a subtle slight moving of the hands and pivoting of hips and legs.

We waited for more of the alarming shrieks. I began to ascend the foreboding staircase. Luther was not too far behind. My heart at this point was racing.

Wesley Thornton spoke up in an insistent manner as I my foot hit the second step. "Officers, there is no need for your present stance. Amora has two female cats, neither of them is fixed. There are times their beastly scuffles make a wallop of disturbing noises."

We stood there waiting on a repeat of that haunting set of noises. Ten minutes went by, nothing. Wesley Thornton spoke up in a breathy whisper. "Are you two done with being on guard duty? Amora has two female cats, not spayed either one. Sometimes they get into a beastly ruckus once in a while."

I wanted to ask more questions. By the expression of the butler, we had worn out our welcome. I was beginning to entertain thoughts we would be back to this estate repeatedly despite our icy reception.

Without missing a beat turning left onto a crowded street, Luther pulled out onto North Meridian Street. "Did you believe the butler's explanation for that noise up in the Tower?"

"Not for a minute. Both Rathbone and Wesley Thornton are hiding something major. They knew we didn't have a search and seizure court order. Here we are, a threat of some FBI agents taking over our case, and a house full of secrets we can't get near." I said, shrugging my shoulders. "We have entered an investigation in untraveled waters."

"I hate to suggest this." Luther said.

"Go ahead. I'm ready for anything you might come up with."

"Well, Glenda, you have this obvious interest in Amado Rathbone. Get close to him, and you might get some ideas on how we can proceed despite those agents at the division."

"I tried at Unc's one night, falling flat on my charming butt."

"Althea was told about a talk at Hartung Hall in the auditorium from her boss at St. Vincent's Mental Health Center. Your growing crush is giving a lecture on the Anderson University campus Tuesday night next week." Luther filled me in on one way to proceed.

"So, you're saying, show up looking alluring within reason. Try on a little undercover tactic. Why not!" I expressed, showing reluctant compliance.

Monday morning circumstances were defined to both my partner and I as, 'it is what it is'. We were introduced to a four-person team: three male agents and one female. They came on to us as very stiff, unfriendly, indifferent, and quite robotic.

With an unspoken agreement, Luther and I gave over what we had compiled in the last six weeks. What we already knew and what we were about to do was saved also on files in our respective computers in our residences.

Luther was surprisingly approved for a short vacation from our sergeant. I'm sure Althea was so thrilled, she would not question why he did this. I was content to be at Mitch Gable's beck and call for surveillance with one of the other detectives at the various farms where there had been reports of savage killings of livestock.

Tuesday evening brought with it a nervousness I had not experienced since prom back in my senior year in high school. In order not to alarm Amado of my sudden appearance, I came into the auditorium with Melanie Rossen. I agreed wholeheartedly to wait with Melanie for Manny and Amado.

Amado's reaction to my presence proved to be much different than that night at Unc's when my electricity was out. His smile directed at me made him more charming than our first meeting at Bobber's Café. Manny suggested the four of us grab some dinner at Melanie and his favorite restaurant, Vera Mae's Bistro in Muncie.

With Amado and Manny's shared taste for the gourmet side of dining, I agreed to meet them at the restaurant, downtown Muncie on East Jackson St. This type of restaurant ran on reservations only, but Professor Foy possessed a carte blanche status. The twenty-minute drive was sufficient time for the maître di' to prepare a table for four.

Right away I spied an empty chair next to Amado which I gladly took. I leaned in close to his left ear to ask. "What do you recommend? I'm more of a meat and potato gal."

"I believe you would enjoy the shepherd's pie. Our family butler rates that dish as his personal favorite." He answered me almost coming close to kissing distance. His breath smelled of peppermint and white chocolate.

"By the way, my partner and I met your butler when we came to interview your father." I added to see if he would become squirmy by my statement.

"When was that?"

"Last Friday, we were following up on a lead." I answered, still he seemed calm and very charming.

Before offering any kind of reply, he noticed the waiter coming closer to our table. He ended our close exchange by asking Melanie something. "Melanie, are you partial to shepherd's pie?"

"Oh, Yes, the shepherd's pie is the only dish I order." She answered laughing over at my adjacent direction. "You will love the way they prepare it. The combination of mashed potatoes on top, carrots, onions, celery and the tender beef underneath is delicious."

Amado ordered a dish I was embarrassed to admit seemed a total gag, but I held back using any disgusting noises. I offered instead a curiosity to know more about what he ordered. I sat there intently listening to how Amado instructed the waiter on every detail of his order.

"What in the sweetbread category do you have?"

The waiter thought for a couple of minutes, then answered Amado. "Sir, we have the pancreas in calf or lamb."

"I will have the lamb pancreas, searing on each side for only brief amount of minutes." Amado instructed in his precise manner of speaking.

Showing my complete ignorance, I asked. "What in heaven's name is this sweetbread?"

Manny offered a brief explanation. "Basically sweetbreads are offal. Pluck or organ meats referring to the internal organs and entrails of a butchered animal."

"Is it any good? It sounds like eating something on a dare like the Filipino balut I tried." I said with a look of horror.

Melanie interjected. "Glenda, you've been doing your homework. You know about balut!"

"Sure do. I took the plunge last Friday from an Asian restaurant outside of Chicago. To look at its outward appearance it was horrid. It tasted like cheese and toasted oysters." I said, looking over at Amado.

He showed no sign of uneasiness. Instead of continuing on with the table-talk discussion of balut, Amado offered his take on sweetbreads. "Sweetbreads taste richer and sweeter than muscle meats you are used to, Glenda. In France and Italy, chefs serve them in a rich smooth brown sauce. I prefer less roasting with no sauce." He took my hand as he finished talking. Something I wasn't expecting at all. It felt nice.

His affection heightened as I agreed to drop him off at the Hartung Hall parking lot. His black sleek Lexus was waiting for him. We made some lame bit of small talk. He interrupted my ramblings about how I entered the police academy at such a young age by an alarming set of passionate kisses, pushing me up against the driver's side of his car.

His lips drew me in so hard. I thought I was to fall into a dead faint. My conscious mind was fogged up by a growing passion for him. Suddenly as forceful as he grabbed me to him, he pulled me away so hard I almost tripped onto the asphalt lot.

"Glenda, I can't love you the way your lips are speaking to me. I'm cursed to fail at performing like the man you so desire. I couldn't help myself when you were trying so hard to be clever tonight. You are so lovely, and so raw in the way you talk." He told me, then slipped quickly into his car.

On the lonely dark parking lot, I was left with confusion and disgust in myself to totally lose any sensibility I had when Luther and I agreed to get closer to him. That night, I tossed and turned in bed. I tried to make sense of what he said. '*I'm cursed to fail at performing like the man you so desire.*'

His statement rolled over and over in my mind, *cursed to fail at performing like the man you so desire.* My first definition of what he meant was: he was impotent. To my way of thinking, the professional I prided myself to be—just as well.

Although his strong kisses translated, he knew how to charge up my sexual barometer. Intimacy had always been a problem to me. When a man knew how to kiss me, puff up my inner desire as well as my lips made me jelly in his hands. Coming back to his mysterious declaration in the parking lot, lovemaking with this alluring man seemed to be at a far reach.

Knowing my partner as I do, the table talk over sweetbreads could prove useful. I had a mental image of those sweetbreads on Amado's plate—well on the raw side, in color and texture. Witnessing many autopsies, I began to think Amado's taste in food defined to be on the peculiar side.

Chapter Seven

Althea's Run

Althea Roberts to anyone who would first lay eyes on, was an African-American beauty possessing a high caliber of physical attributes bestowed upon a dark statuesque Nubian princess type. In meeting her at Indiana University Bloomington campus, Luther Charles was surprised to find Althea a psychology major, not the field he thought she would go for.

They parted when she went off to graduate school in Missouri while he took his degree in criminal justice to the police academy in Culver, Indiana. Their strong connection as undergrads stayed true for both of them. When they crossed paths in Anderson, they both were well established in their respective career choices.

I had met Althea at certain times double-dating when Luther and I became partners four years ago. She was gracious to me only because of Luther. If I had met her in passing on the street or shopping at the local grocery store, she would ignore me. A mere 'Hello' was something she would rather not do.

It was getting close to early evening, but seeing it was middle August the night sky was hours away. Althea looked in on Luther glued to his computer screen. To let him know she was going out for a run seemed futile in his present state of cyber-hypnosis.

Luther and Althea had purchased a split level retro home built in the 1950s on North Shore Blvd. eighteen months ago. It didn't take too long she would enter the woods which lined the first nine holes at Grandview Golf Course. Her six-mile run took her along the dense nature trail on what was called the 'back nine' then she would turn close to the Anderson Municipal Plant. She turned again to continue on the 'front nine' of the golf course.

Halfway through the passage in the heavy woods, she went over in her mind the late night pillow-talk Luther and her engaged in on his recent case. In her years of internship before The Richmond Mental Hospital closed for good, she experienced how far a human would go for his or her propensity for evil.

Two weeks ago at breakfast, Luther pressed her to give him her thoughts on the fantasy implications of this case. "Well, baby, if you must know. The 83% of those Filipinos and Asians who believe in this bizarre legend are merely having faith in nothing more than centuries-evolved superstitions. This deranged delusional assailant has fully taken on the legend in every detail to gain an inner sensation of power to be fed for the sake of others frailness and fear."

She shook her head in the direction of the dreary battleship gray municipal plant ahead. She talked out loud to herself, "my Luther going to research his way to a visitation to the mental health center taking that partner of his with him."

She stopped to stretch her arms, legs and go down to twenty-five squats. Knowing the squats were a preview to her preparing her womb for the inevitable labor in four months. She went through cleansing breaths with each squat, stroking on her small baby bump.

She heard a ticking sound, could not distinguish the repetitive sounds from loud ticks of crickets among the high blades of dry grass around her, or to the ticking similar to their bedroom alarm clock. She looked up at the sky. The sun was disappearing behind the dense tree foliage meeting the muted lavender navy blue sky.

In her haste to entertain the need to complete a routine run, she had failed to take a bathroom break before setting on. Althea looked around, behind and ahead of where she stood. No one to see her drop her designer wear exercise pants. She relieved herself and took a leaf or two to wipe herself.

She decided to turn back through the woods with the sky getting darker. Through the trees she could see the White River moving slowly as a night breeze set in. She heard the ticking sound again. It seemed louder as if it was coming closer to her overhead.

Sharp blade-like feet clamped onto her shoulders. She was taken up to the sky above the tops of the tall trees. She attempted to look up to see her captor, but the noise and shadow of flying netting blocked visibility. An agonizing pain on each shoulder took over her consciousness of realizing the clamping blades were tearing into her skin like she was a piece of meat hanging from butcher's clamps.

She was lowered to an embankment along the river. First she was on her stomach, then the blade-like fingers flipped her over to face the one who had her in its vice-grip. By this moment whatever fear she felt was overrode by her seething anger of someone having the audacity to disturb her sacred run. When she saw a tube-like crimson tongue coming out of the creature's open mouth, her mind went over what Luther had told her of the fate of the victims.

She pulled out a vial of liquid garlic mixed with salt Luther had insisted she carry at all times. The contents of the vial were strategically doused on the tip of the tongue, moving down to her bare abdomen. She thought, *you're not going to kill my baby!*

The garlic liquid and salt mixture caused the creature to repel back. In anger, its mouth full of razor-sharp fangs clamped down onto Althea's left side inches from her mid-section housing her growing child. Althea bellowed in a deep guttural cry so loud someone walking in front of the entrance to the clubhouse and restaurant would hear her scream.

Suddenly, she heard gunshots very close. The creature let loose of her lower left side. She heard a loud flutter of wings through her agonizing pain. Luther's heavy breath was soon felt on the top of her head. Breathing hard, and crying rare tears of knowing her husband was at hand, she heard his breathless voice.

"Baby, I've got you." Luther assured Althea he was at her side.

Holding her hand with his left, with his right index finger he hit the keyboard three times on his iPhone, 911. His voice breathless, he said, " 911, I have a victim of a violent attack in the woods behind the entrance of the Grandview Golf Course clubhouse and restaurant. This is Detective Luther Charles, APD Detective Division. Our precise location is on the west side embankment along White River."

Althea, her hands bloodied from trying to stop the bleeding stroked his face, "You were right. I thought you were being influenced by Glenda. Luther, I'm so sorry. He didn't get near the baby…" She passed out due to shock and the pain. Luther ripped part of his shirt to make a sash round her middle to stop the bleeding.

The detective Mitch assigned to me had contracted food poisoning the night before. I grabbed a cup of coffee before going out to Markleville on my own. The female FBI agent showed up at the opening of the break room as I was pouring my coffee.

"I got a look at you and your partner's very revealing chart. The speculative profile of your assailant is something I know a great deal about." She told me, leaning up against the door molding.

I looked her over, not in an interested party manner. I wished to know who I was dealing with. She was my height, 5 foot, 8 inches. Her facial features did not match her fair complexion with a wide flatter nose much like Luther's nose. She had a curious scattering of freckles on her high cheekbones.

In full fight mode, my voice raised, I said, "Look! I've got a lame interview with some pig farmer in Markleville. I'm in no mood to listen to your derisions of our findings!"

"No derision or scoff, this is a friendly observation. You gave a name to something I was told as a child, that hard as I try cannot forget. Let's start over, Detective McMahan. I'm Wyla Stark. My grandmother is Filipina originally from the island of Panay." She got closer, offering her hand as a gesture of cease-fire.

"Sorry, your presence and the other agents have caused me to be on the defensive big time. It is the nature of speculation in this case that is kind of making me crazy." I said, shaking her hand.

"I get it more than you could realize. Do you mind if I tag along?" Wyla offered.

"I guess. Mind you, I will probably attempt to pick your brain since you have Filipino heritage." I was inwardly grateful for someone who seemed to be an ally but I didn't let her know that.

The Painter Farm was located between the small towns of Emporia and Markleville. Both towns got on the map due to the importance of Red Gold Tomato Corporation, the center point. I drove down Columbus Avenue giving us access to Highway 36.

I did not waste any time. "So, Wyla, tell me more about your grandmother."

"How much time do we have until we reach the farm?" She asked.

"Oh, a good twenty-five minutes."

"Okay, I'll see how far I can go with my introduction to what makes you crazy. My grandmother came from the province of Capiz, rich in the fishing trade on the island of Panay. I read from your chart, you are fully aware most in the islands think Capiz is the home of this mysterious shapeshifter. The account my grandmother told me about makes it difficult for me to say the name out loud. You must understand those of us with any ties to the islands are superstitious. Even me with my law enforcement training. Maybe that is why I went into this type of work, to get away from mysterious accounts and supernatural ways in the Philippines." Wyla stopped for some strange reason.

"What's the matter?" I asked.

"Before I continue, I want to know I'm not opening up to someone who isn't serious about seeing the case all the way through even when it gets to the point of being beyond the fringe." Wyla said.

"What do you mean about beyond the fringe?"

"Beyond the fringe of sanity," continued Wyla. "There exists a madness that accompanies anyone who truly pursues the phenomena we are talking about. One of the reasons why I have been running from it."

Wyla threw her head back and laughed. "So ironic, I have walked into the legend here in the Midwest of all places!"

I slowed down, and looked at her intently. "Wyla, I'm not backing off. I meant crazy, because I met someone who might fit the criteria. His beauty and grace of style makes it hard for me to resist his charm. Almost impossible to get my head around the fact of this gorgeous man turning into such a monster. I could use some real help in gathering more evidence or even instincts on who this could be. I'm emotionally invested as well as factually invested."

Wyla continued, getting somewhat technical. "This attacker you have profiled is a visceral sucker known specifically, because of a ticking sound labeled, 'Tik-Tik'. It's preference for a kill is the growing fetus, but when that is denied somehow it eats the entrails, internal organs of a human or animal. This thing as the islands tell of it, the aswang has various types and the ability to shape shift, in the daytime hours appearing as a large pig or dog. What we are dealing with has powers of the black art of witchcraft and at times possesses the unthinkable desire for human flesh."

"Sorry to interrupt. So, you are saying this thing when manifested has tendencies to go for cannibalism?" I had to ask. She gave me a look that I had not taken seriously when she spoke about the power and eerie mystery of this assailant. I have always had a delayed reaction to things explained to me on the outlandish nature. My mind was a sponge otherwise I would not be able to sort tedious details of cases coming my way. This particular case and the knowledge Wyla possessed did hit the mind vault. My mind recorded every gory strange detail, not to forget when needed to be brought forth in the future.

"Remind me when we are in a more stationary place to give you a first-hand account of this creature when my grandmother was only eight. When I talked about madness, this account will open a portal to the supernatural that you wish you would have not heard. It looks to me, we have arrived at this farm. I'll continue later."

We pulled into the farm's gravel path to the house. What was going around in my mind hearing this account from Wyla had to be put on hold. Both of us were forced to put on our respective professional faces of cool analytical police officers for this interview with Mr. Painter. My head was spinning with the strangeness of this case as each victim cemented the folklore legend of the aswang, which could actually be something so horrible walking among us. My skepticism on the night I interviewed the first victim was slowly disappearing making way for an open mind ready to convert to the supernatural legend.

Chapter Eight
Emergency Interrupts

The farmhouse, an American Salt-box style two-story appeared to have had a significant face lift. The light celery green paint job with stark white trim on the vinyl siding and window treatments complemented well with the surrounding shades of green from the dense woods.

I knocked on the front door to see a tall rotund white-haired man in gray overalls and a white T-shirt underneath open the door. He came outside to bring us around a large concrete-block structure. It held a number of enclosures for his various pigs and larger hogs in hay-filled mud-splattered quarters.

The overall odor of pig waste and damp hay both of us got used to. When we came to the last enclosure larger than any of the others, breathing became difficult. There was a strong pervading stench of overall decay.

"See it for yourself, detectives. This prize hog I had to forfeit from the Indiana State Fair. Serena had been responsible for the renovation on my house you drove up to. I found her last night after being wakened from a noise I wouldn't want my worst enemy to hear." The farmer told us, then spit out a wad of chewed tobacco onto the ground mashed down in hay and damp mud.

The sight of the enormous hog was like nothing I had ever seen, mess of half-eaten organs and hay mixed with dried blood. Wyla took a bandana from her jacket pocket, placed it over her nose and mouth. She walked into the pen with no appearance of trepidation. She moved slow and methodical as she examined torn organs from various lower parts of the hog.

She motioned me to get closer inside the enclosure. I flinched as I took off my jacket and used it to cover my nose and mouth. Wyla pointed with an eraser tip of a pencil to a ravaged area of what I assumed to be the liver and pancreas. I nodded in understanding of what she had said about entrails during our drive to the farm. When we moved out of the enclosure I could not get over the timing of our conversation in the car to the findings from Mr. Painter's prize hog.

All of us walked back to the front door where we first met the disillusioned farmer. Painter directed his question to Wyla. "What in the name of Christ did this? I can't imagine a bobcat or a coyote doing this!"

"Mr. Painter, what was left of the entrails confirms the same kind of assailant who attacked our growing list of victims in the Anderson area has now ventured out into surrounding Madison County." Wyla told him.

"What the hell do I do now? You people are known to take years to solve this serial type of crimes!" The farmer bellowed out.

Wyla said in a cold calculated manner with not much comfort or guarantee this assailant might not come back. "I suggest to you to purchase those bags of ice used for the Indiana winters to be scattered in circle formations around your house and the enclosures you keep your livestock in. I know for a fact this type of perpetrator is repelled by salt and will not touch your livestock with the salt paths around them."

Driving back to Anderson, I was impressed with Wyla's coldness. Her reserve appeared to me might stave off any of the madness she mentioned. My creeping mind-meld terrorized me in the solitary hours of a pervading belief system that kept me up at night. I acted manic in the day hours to dig deeper into this legend. I wanted so much to be like a cooler frame of mind demonstrated by Wyla.

Halfway back to Anderson, Wyla declared a curious contradiction after we had been exposed to such a gross mess of flesh. "I'm hungry for seafood, but please, not Red Lobster."

"I know a place you would like. Besides, it is not too far from the site where the first victim was attacked."

"Melanie Rossen, she was forthcoming when the other agents interviewed her yesterday. One of my fellow agents asked her if she was determined to stick to her previous account. She became very cross with him and politely asked us to leave her office at the university." Wyla said, showing an amused expression.

At Bobber's Café there were plenty of tables to take inside. I thought to myself, *the newspapers sure did a number on previous diners to keep them away. They had been spooked, not knowing the two basic truths: our supernatural attacker would not show up in the daytime or would only attack a woman alone in a remote area.*

Katie Fisher came up to our booth by the series of windows with a view of the pier and lake. "Detective McMahan, welcome back."

"Katie, nice to see you again. This is Agent Stark, she is giving me some special knowledge of this case." I said with a full smile.

"What is your daily special?" Wyla asked.

"Well, we got in some mountain trout yesterday from Colorado. It is grilled and comes with a house salad and twice-baked potato." Katie was happy to offer with her usual cheerful demeanor.

"Glenda, that's sounds what I just had in mind. Are you in?" I nodded wholeheartedly. "Katie, dear, we will have two." Wyla instructed.

"You know you were a pretty cool customer at the farm. I thought I always had a strong stomach. What was left of that hog I'm afraid I will see in my dreams, if I can sleep tonight." I told Wyla, while drinking almost all of my ice water.

"What I've seen since coming to the FBI has made me impervious to the worst of crime scenes. Except for the corpses of little children. Once, I went on an investigation five years ago of four children, or what was left of them hanging from meat hooks in a hot still-air shack where tobacco farmers hung their bunches of leaves. The mother had found them. I not only lost my breakfast but horrible recurring images of them haunted me in the night hours for weeks." Wyla told, visibly shuddering with her neck and shoulders.

"That had to have been so rough. I've been in police work since I graduated from high school. When I saw Evie Fortner's body at the burial mound at Mounds Park, that had to be defined as my most eerie image to date."

"Wow, you're still a youth in this grisly business called public service. Looks to me, you're in your early thirties? Yeah!" Wyla said.

"Precisely, I'm thirty-two. Can I ask? Are you in your thirties?" I asked, but felt pensive about the question.

"I'm on the tail end of the my thirties, going to be thirty-nine in December," she informed me not showing any irritation.

Katie brought our salads. Wyla looked up smiling. "Katie, I've got a question. The noises coming from the embankment not too far from this restaurant. Did they sound in any way human?"

"No, they didn't. Even when Lester and I heard those sounds of that black kind of bird shooting up into the night sky. It's real hard to describe, gives me chills whenever I go back in my mind. There among the screams of a woman, there was a loud ticking like a bomb." Katie answered, showing to be somewhat spooked going over it again for Wyla.

Wyla patted her on her right arm. "Dear, I'm getting what you're saying. Forgive my switching the subject. Can I have a coffee? Please."

It was baffling to me how Wyla could switch a grim subject of some supernatural being to such a natural inclination for a cup of coffee. I guess, she was only defined by her station in life to identification of a FBI agent, and nothing more.

Katie obeyed without delay. We dove into our luncheon salads like two women who had not eaten in days. We sat there devouring our salads and then on to our entrees, exchanging expressions of sheer delight in the amazing flavors of lake fish perfectly seasoned and prepared.

Taking an after-lunch breather, we took in the sun reflected on the glassy lake from our window vista view. Suddenly my cell phone vibrated in my left pant-pocket. It was Luther, I think. His voice sounded so strange. It was low almost a whisper and quite solemn.

"Glenda, I'm here at Community with Althea. That thing got her last night. We are on the third floor, corner, Room 321."

"Oh, my God! We'll be right there." I shouted, not saying who I was with as if Luther would have given a rat's ass.

"Wyla, Luther's fiancé is victim No. 20. We've got to get to the hospital." I told her in a breathless manner. My insides rolled around in a combination of intense shock and seething anger. This was getting personal.

"By all means. I'll leave a fifty for the entrees and a tip."

Katie came out of the kitchen as we were getting ready to open the entrance door. Wyla shouted out to her, "Katie, we've got an emergency. We left you the money for the lunches and a tip. It's on the table."

When we arrived at Althea's private room, Luther was standing outside the closed door. I came up to him, holding onto his shoulders. "It can't be true. Dare I ask!"

"By her quick thinking, he wasn't able to harm the baby." Luther said, reassuring me to the fact the baby was still safe and undisturbed. He shook his head, showing his infamous half-grin which created a dimple close to the corner of his mouth.

He went on. "After the many times she fought against carrying the vial of garlic and salt liquid. She used it!"

Luther looked behind me to see Wyla. "What's she doing here?"

"Luther, she's an ally! Believe it, we got back from Markleville. Another victim, this time a prize hog. Oh, this is Agent Wyla Stark." I informed him.

He nodded to Wyla, and said. "Sorry, it's been a damn nightmare! The doctor is with her now. I am all nerves and anger…" He broke down in my arms and cried.

The doctor came to where were standing. Luther looked at him, nodding his head while the doctor was speaking to him. My partner left and went into Althea's room. I recognized the doctor to be Dr. Reyes who had treated Rosa Montez.

"Doctor, I'm Detective Charles's partner. This is FBI Agent Wyla Stark. How's Althea?" I shouted at the doctor as he was making his way back to the nurses' station.

He stopped and turned around to us. He approached me and said. "Well, you probably already know the baby was not harmed. Although her assailant ate away part of Althea's liver. We found out in surgery we were able to reconnect the delicate tissue to the existing liver. She will be compromised to a less fatty diet and no consuming of anything alcoholic."

"Having treated Rosa Montez and being Filipino yourself, you have head knowledge of this cursed manifestation. Does this 'Tik-Tik' normally stalk a victim on purpose? It had to know she was connected to Detective Charles!" Wyla probed without a bit of diplomacy.

"I will say this. This type of phenomenon you refer to at the time of its transformation does not have a clear way of thinking the way humans do. They do not know what they are doing only to stop the burning inside and quench the thirst for their ultimate feed whether it be a developing fetus or the entrails of an animal or human. I've got to go!" Dr. Reyes stressed to us standing there.

Wyla came over to me, "Tell you what, Glenda. I'm going to check in with the other agents. Go ahead and visit inside. I'll catch up with you later."

I slowly entered the room. Luther was seated on the other side of the bed, holding onto Althea's arm. "Hey, you two. I wanted to see how you were doing. I'll understand if you don't want me in here."

Althea turned her head. She spoke to Luther, "Baby, before I go back to sleep. Let me have a word with Glenda."

"Sit down, Glenda. I've got something to say." Althea said in her authoritative way. Her penetrating stare made me feel uncomfortable.

"Before this happened, I thought Luther was getting his crazy conclusions about this supernatural perpetrator from your infamous unrealistic instincts. I saw that thing for real. More than me, Luther has had the wind knocked out of him. Do everything in your power to pursue it and rid this community of it before the monster goes further and murders countless unsuspecting women." Althea said, in a surprising eloquent way. She came off as if she trusted me to pull off this tall order.

This was the most she had ever spoken to me at one sitting. For once, maybe she approved of me but with a condition. The task had always held ominous conditions but now it went into full-throttle killer mode of do it or I will have Althea's wrath on my head.

Chapter Nine

Girls Talk Turkey

I met Wyla in the surgery waiting area. She must have deciphered from the wild look I had plastered on my face. I needed a stiff drink. "You don't look so good. Can I buy you a drink?"

"What about your fellow agents?"

"They have decided to pack it in for the night at your local Hampton Inn. None of the victims from your list will talk to them." Wyla told me, giggling under her breath.

"I've got the place, and it won't cost you a dime. Hope you don't mind my apartment, only a few blocks from where your rental is parked at the APD parking lot."

We walked up the back steps of my landlady's vintage 1889 Victorian three-story home. I unlocked my door and let us both in from the small foyer. Wyla walked around peeking into my kitchen, then moving slowly to my front room. She studied through my lined up books from my three bookshelves. She glanced over my collection of classic horror novels, Stephen King novels and Dan Brown books.

She made her way over to my mini-bar close to my entertainment center. Bending down searching for something to drink she rummaged through my collection of hard liquor. She lifted up a bottle of Glenfiddich scotch whiskey.

"You're a boozer. This is cracking fine malt whiskey!" She said. Hearing a slight accent, I got curious.

"Where did that accent come from?"

"My father is first generation Scot. That's the reason for my freckles and light skin. Sure you realize, Filipinos are considered brown-skinned people."

"Oh, that's right. Your grandmother from the Philippines would mean your mother is Filipina. Sorry, for my westernized ignorance."

"Indeed, part Filipina and Spanish, with me coming to be a real mutt," Wyla said, then stared at the bottle again. "Can I break it open?"

"Why not. I need something strong. There's glasses on the top shelf of the bar. I'll get some ice." I said, going into my kitchen.

Wyla took a whiff from the opening, "My, my, I wouldn't have guessed someone your age would know the finest of scotches unless you have moonlighted as a bartender."

"That's my Grandpa Pete who raised me. I got that bottle last year for Christmas." I told her, settling in on an easy chair across from my purple sofa. Wyla took to the sofa, immediately after I gave her a glass of the malt with sufficient ice.

I plopped down across from her, visually enjoying the scotch. "So, I think this is the appropriate time to give me your grandmother's account when she was eight."

"Well, my great-grandfather had been on a month-long fishing expedition in deep waters. He came home late one night, a very hot stifling night. My great-grandmother was seven months along with another child, waiting up for her husband. My grandmother, Caralyn heard doors being slammed, shouting coming from the back of the house. She had been sleeping in one of the back bedrooms with her grandmother. The grandmother heard the noticeable sounds getting louder and more frequent. There was one noise only known to Caralyn's grandmother—a screeching blood-curdling sound. She gathered Caralyn into her arms and held her tight on her bed where underneath, a large slab of dry ice was setting in a pan. This was a way to repel the aswang from getting into their bedroom. Caralyn's grandmother knew one of her parents or the both of them had perished under that creature of evil. In the morning, they went out to the outside of the house where they saw Caralyn's father putting something large into his pickup truck." Wyla said, then picked up her glass to top off the contents.

"What happened to Caralyn's mother?" I asked.

"She had been killed along with the child by this aswang, the locals called manananggal. My great-grandfather had cut the creature in pieces with a machete, he kept in the kitchen pantry. He had buried his wife and child, then disposed of the creature." Wyla finished her story with a noticeable shudder with her head and shoulders.

She sat there on the couch, her eyes staring down onto the area rug. I wanted to say something but feeling it would be rude somehow—I stayed silent. She put her glass on the coffee table in front of her. In an instant her face and body language went back to her usual analytical posture, and opened her mouth.

"So, give me a name of this elusive savage assailant we are pursuing. You must have it rolling around in your head after so many victims." Wyla said, probing as was her nature to do.

It wasn't hard for me to respond. Drinking down the contents of my glass, my tongue was sufficiently loosened to break the code of silence until there was more evidence. "Amora Rathbone, heir to the million-dollar Big Pharma dynasty in Indiana. She's very aloof and quite mysterious, fits the profile so far with the icing on the cake of her mother being from the Philippines and sister to Amado Rathbone. One alarming thing, her eyes changed colors at our first meeting, setting me very uneasy."

Wyla lifted up her glass and said. "Oh, Yeah, two names that made that infamous chart of yours. Why do you think she fits our mysterious legend?"

" Luther and I had an interview at the Rathbone estate with the corporate head Ethan, father to Amora and Amado. Again, those dark brown eyes turned to red. I was rattled but attempted to talk to her all the same. She gave me the silent treatment. As we had finished with the father, Luther and I heard a strange unnerving noises coming from the drafty stone staircase leading to the third level of what the butler called The Tower."

Wyla nodded, showing she heard my brief description of that strange morning at the Rathbone's. She got up and poured a small amount of the malt whiskey into her glass. "Tell you what! Let's go back to the Rathbone estate for a cold call. Its very definition of suprise value will catch them off guard."

"Would you be violating your agency's protocol by pairing with me on going outside the lines?" I asked.

"When I was at the hospital, I had a talk with your sergeant Gable. I told him I believed this line-up of severe savage attacks was from a copy-cat. Someone who was from the Philippines or some sick psychopath who possesses full knowledge of the Philippine Lower Mythology which is as you know rampant in the islands." She said, then taking the contents of the glass back, drinking in one gulp.

I shouted in an amusing tone. "He bought that? It does sound believable. Does it bother you to bend your integrity as a law enforcement officer to downright lie?"

"As you continue in this case, you will realize many things. One thing, to bend the truth so the case can go forward, with no stalls." Wyla told me, lowering her eyelids for emphasis.

Wyla made her way to the door. I told her. "I can drive you back to your car."

She lifted up her jacket. Pointing to her firearm resting in her shoulder holster. I realized she would be fine on her own. I waved good night.

The next morning, I drove up to the familiar walled gate. I pushed the red call button on the silver intercom. A man's voice spoke. "Who goes there? I say."

I recognized the voice to be Wesley Thornton. "Wesley, this is Detective McMahan from the APD with FBI agent Wyla Stark. We are in need of talking to one of the Rathbones."

"I regret your troublesome morning commute. You've failed to make a proper appointment." He clicked off.

I raised my voice to emphasize the importance of our unexpected visit. "I respect that. I have this special agent who needs to interview a Rathbone in the worst way. I believe her station in law enforcement takes some weight, especially in this being a cold call."

"I will open the gate."

Wyla and I looked at each other about ready to burst into laughter, but we needed to keep a serious composure. She took in the majesty of the grounds as I drove slowly down the paved path to the half-moon shaped driveway.

"Where's the Tower you spoke of?" She asked before we got out of my car.

"It's behind the double chimneys to the left," I pointed. "Do you see the top of the American flag blowing? The flag is attached to the turret's spire."

Wesley Thornton opened the door as I was about to knock. "Detective McMahan, you and Agent Stark go on into Master Ethan's office. I'm sure you remember the way."

We walked passed the stone staircase leading to the Tower's third level. Wyla let out a whelp, "What a draft or I should say, gust of cold air! They must have a heck of an energy bill."

"Well, the draft from up there going to the Tower is the quarters of Amado and Amora. The butler did not tell me the reason for frigid air you are feeling. He only said, they prefer the coldness to the moderate air in the other parts of the house." I explained.

Wyla walked around the spacious perimeter of Ethan's office. "My, my, this rich décor reminds me of a lord's drawing room in the UK."

"So, you've been to Britain?" I asked.

"Sometimes this job requires crossing the Atlantic for leads," said Wyla. She gave me a factious wink.

A familiar voice greeted us as he walked in an elegant regal manner to his father's massive desk. "Well, well, how have I rated a visit from an auspicious member of the FBI?"

I spoke up. "Amado, I wasn't expecting you! This is Agent Wyla Stark. She's been giving me a hand while Luther is on leave. His fiancé has become victim No. 20."

He lowered his eyes, moving closer to Wyla. He pulled out his right hand as a polite gesture to shake her hand. "Agent Stark, it is a pleasure. I'm Amado Rathbone, son to Ethan who I presume you wanted to speak to."

"Actually, we wanted to speak to your sister, Amora." Wyla moved closer, nose to nose. "Hmmm, have you been to the eye doctor, Mr. Rathbone?"

"I see. You came all this way from Anderson to ask about an eye condition." Amado said, standing his ground with no nervousness apparent on his face or body.

"Your eyes are dilated. Which gives me two reasons to explain. Either you are using some kind of narcotic, or you've been to the eye doctor for some reason."

"Madam, as of late I've been going on a line of meds that my doctor administered." Amado answered her.

"What medical condition are you being treated for?" Wyla persisted with her take of what was going on with his eyes.

"Well, Agent Stark, you are treading on the path that wholly belongs to HIPPA. To answer your question as you persist in, my physician would have to be present."

I interjected. "Come on, you two, this battle-of-the-wills is getting us nowhere. Amado, as Wyla mentioned we came to speak to Amora. Where is she?"

"Not even in our office at Saxony. Amora is in the twin cities for a month of group sessions for our new drug, 'Divinia'." Amado said, turning to me with a warm smile.

For the next few minutes there came an uncomfortable silence like a stifling blanket of humid air difficult to catch one's breath. I looked over at Wyla who kept glaring at Amado. He put his hands into his jean pockets glaring at her in the same destructive manner. My breathing became labored so much I made a move towards the open office door.

"Wyla, why don't we move on." She didn't want to budge. "I insist, I'm having trouble breathing!" I pleaded.

Wyla raised up her arms, "I guess! Detective McMahan, you get your way."

I drove out onto North Meridian Street, thankful in the consistent flow of traffic. Wyla scolded me. "Why did you wimp out on me?"

"I wasn't kidding about not being able to breath! Seriously, what was going on in that office scared the crap out of me." I revealed.

Wyla nodded, beginning to get something clear in her mind. "You think our suspect is Amora. Well, missy, he was using some downright kind of witchcraft on you while him and I were having that enjoyable staring contest. I think our suspect is him, not his sister."

"Another trait of the mysterious legend, witchcraft pops up!" I surmised, blurting it out as we got onto Binford Ave. taking us to Interstate 69.

Wyla threw her head back and laughed, then filled me in on what she was doing. "I was playing 'bad cop' while you naturally acted as the 'good cop'. You need to shake off your school-girl crush with him. It is really obvious, and could make you powerless as we get closer to his real identity."

This FBI agent with a strong connection to the ancient legend unfolding in fast action was to be my exit into the seventeen-year comfort zone I had existed in. The APD Detective Division or for that matter the whole of this country seldom experienced a case so bizarre, so rampant with a succession in terror. I found myself going by her every direction in many facets of our ongoing investigation.

Chapter Ten

There Came A Lull

As Wyla and I concentrated our efforts on the pertinent research for the IndyMerck facility of Saxony, there appeared to be two weeks of no victims found. The other three agents concentrated on finding out the progress of Rathbone's new drug, Divinia.

Wyla joined me in the break room for lunch. The other agents she referred to as John, Paul, and George had brought in from Scampy's—12-inch supreme pizza and Stromboli sandwiches. I ogled over the taste of the Stromboli. "How did they know about Scampy's best sandwich?"

"These three had filled me in on the best places in Anderson to eat, especially the places that aren't widely known." Wyla said, taking another slice.

"Why do you call them, John, Paul, and George?"

"I call them those names for two reasons. One, they are all originally from Liverpool, England. Second reason, they have the same haircuts as The Beatles did when they came to the U.S. in 1964." She said, chuckling. Not a response I would imagine coming from a high-powered FBI agent. I rather liked the fact, she could be amused easily.

We finished our high-caloric lunch by chasing down a more sensible beverage of bottled Dasani waters. "Glenda, how close have you gotten to sexy-looking Amado?"

"Well, I got real close on two occasions. I brushed closely with him at a neighborhood bar where he told me he was attracted to me. Another time, I joined him for dinner with the first victim and her longtime boyfriend at a trendy bistro in Muncie. We kissed, pretty heavy exchange on both our parts." I told her. My face getting flushed when I mentioned our kisses.

She gave me a half-ass grin as girlfriends do when talking about strong exchanges between a potential crush. She was all ears as I remembered something I thought was really peculiar about him.

"He ordered sweetbreads, and went through a very detailed explanation on how he wanted his order prepared."

"Which organ of the animal did he order?" Wyla asked. I was impressed with her knowledge of the gourmet offal dish.

"He told the waiter to sear the pancreas of the calf lightly on each side with no breading. I couldn't help but gag when the waiter brought it to him. The color of the calf's internal organ was a fleshy-pink, not something I found very appetizing." I said, visibly shaking with my head and shoulders.

"Mmmm, quite the turn-off on a dinner date. This description does give my theory on Amado some strength." Wyla pointed, raising her voice. "And, this has great bearing on what happened to Luther's fiancé. He couldn't get what he wanted, so he went for her liver, instead."

As both of us experienced our appetites completely sated, the agent with the round silver frames who Wyla called John entered the break room. "Ladies, this is interesting. That group session up in the twin cities happens to be non-existent. The guys and I checked out St. Paul and Minneapolis, every convention center and every educational institution known to hold seminars."

"So much for Amado telling us the truth. I bet he is taking the drug himself. "Wyla said while she was washing her hands.

"John, round up Paul and George to get some solid information on what side effects Divinia is known to have." Wyla turned to him, drying off her hands.

"Sounds good, but there is more. This tidbit of info adds to his lying." John said.

"Well, I'm ready for anything now!" I burst out.

"There was a birth record of Amora, born to Ethan and Divinia Rathbone. There was no record of Amado's birth."

"Oh, great. This news flash from John really confuses me. Who the hell is this Amado?" I asked.

"I believe that is a question for Ethan Rathbone. He won't receive any of us at his home. John, you and the guys track him down at IndyMerck in Indianapolis. Do a cold call which he cannot run from.

"We need some evidence to get a search and seizure order. We've already called the office of Ethan Rathbone. All our calls refused. I fancy a cold call would be thwarted by some efficient secretary." John said, shaking his head.

"Wait, I have an idea. It's outside the police procedure area. Somehow we need to get access to The Tower at the Rathbone estate. I've been wanting to see what it is like up there since Luther and I heard catlike noises coming from the drafty staircase." I suggested with both John and Wyla showing keen interest.

That day, John, Paul and George made a cold call to the office of Ethan Rathbone while Wyla and I put together a plan to get to The Tower quarters. On the drive to the Rathbone estate, we came up with a shaky plan. To park our vehicle close to the residence but away from blocking any driveway. We walked from a convenience store on the corner of 38th Street and North Meridian. Four blocks down on North Meridian Street was the Rathbone gate.

Wyla motioned for me to join her some half-a-mile on the left from the gate where there was a dense area of bushes. We climbed the bushes which took us out of the security range of the butler's intercom system.

In the back part of the house, we both looked at the high and almost impossible climb of The Tower constructed in uneven stone.

Wyla for some reason I did not question had brought a rolled up long parcel of strong rope, the rough kind that hurts while climbing. "Oh, Shit, that is high. Some jutted out stones can help my feet to anchor onto. Well, somehow get over to the front door and pound on the door. Hide when it opens, and watch the butler come out to see if anyone is around. Move quickly and slither in, if you can without him knowing it."

Wyla forgot one matter, pulled on me as I was about to move. "Take this rope. When you get up to where the quarters are, throw the rope down for me to climb up."

I had so many questions rolling around in my head, but failed to ask. I pounded on the door as hard as I could. Like Wyla said, Wesley came to the door. He opened it wide, came out onto the front step, then walked a ways down the path to look around. I had enough time to slip in and run like a bandit to the stone staircase.

With each ascending step, my heart beat harder and faster. The surrounding air got so cold, I could almost see my breath. The hallway was extremely dark and formed in the shape of a large circle constructed in the same configuration of stone work as the outside of the Tower. There were four doors very worn-looking. When I got close to one door, I could see parts of the wood rotted away. I opened the door to a veil of cobwebs so thick as I walked through the spider material had gotten in my hair and all over my clothes. When I got through the unpleasant veil, I saw an altar towards a back wall. There were unlit candles with large globs of dried wax on both sides of a long dark wooden table. In between the candles were framed photographs of women. I got closer and to my amazement recognized every woman in the array of frames.

I looked for a window, there was none. I got out my cellphone to take pictures of the overall altar, then took a photo of each woman. I moved on to the other closed doors. One door was full of metal racks of men and women clothing, wooden shelves full of shoes, undergarments, nightgowns, and hosiery. There was an old fashioned white vanity table and a chair decorated in pink roses in some unique form of metalwork. The last door I went through had to have been the bedroom: an elaborate queen-size bed, end tables with Tiffany-glass lamps and a chaise lounge and to my great relief, a window.

I opened the vertical window to throw Wyla the rope. In a matter of thirty minutes or so, she climbed up for me to drag her into the interior of I assume was Amora's bedroom. "You won't believe what I found." I told her, breathless with excitement. Wyla pushed her hand close to my face. "All in good time."

We walked to the fourth door. We both experienced another see-through curtain of cobwebs. Trying not to cough from the stench, we got deeper into the room. It was bare except for a full-size mattress where there was one sheet, no pillows. There was no other furniture in the room, except for another window to the outside. The odor in the room smelled like stale blood and a lingering breeze of iodine.

We decided to run down the staircase and out the front door. The arrival of us reaching our vehicle did not take too long because of the yelling of Wesley Thornton on the heels of our departure. We got into the car, and I did not hesitate to make our journey back to Anderson.

"Wyla, the first room I entered had an altar with the photos of the women who had been attacked since June. I got pictures on my phone. Take a look."

Wyla went through the display of photographs, all the while, yelling some kind of triumphal yelp. "Well, now we can get a court order for the Saxony facility, Ethan's office, and his children's offices, and one for the estate as well."

"That last room gave me the creeps. Someone must hate their existence so much to live and sleep in such stench and filth, pathetic! I'm more confused though especially about Amado. John told us of no birth certificate for him. In one of the rooms, there were men's clothes: suite jackets, pants, dress shoes, and men's undergarments." I said, shaking in frustration.

"We will get more answers. From the evidence on your phone, Gable must believe we are on to something. Today was a good day, believe it." Wyla said, folding her arms and laying back her head onto the seat.

I was about to say something when my cellphone on the seat close to my thigh vibrated. Now travelling on the straight run to I69, I could pick it up without disturbing the steering. It was Luther.

"Hey, nice surprise! How's things?"

"I'm getting sick of this house, but Althea is getting much better. She's back to her sassy self. She wanted me to ask you to come over for dinner tonight."

"Althea said that, Huh! Yeah! I will. What time?" I answered back somewhat excited. I wanted to share with him about what I took on my phone.

"Get here at 6:30 p.m. Be nice to see your face." He clicked off.

Wyla had me drop her off at The Hampton Inn. The climb up the Tower wore her out. I had enough time to get a shower and put on some clean clothes.

This was the first time I had set foot in Luther and Althea's new home. I shook my head in amusement when I saw a pan filled with steaming dry ice on the front step to the front door. Luther opened the door, showing me in looking casual and quite rested.

The living room was decorated in light wood Mission-style contemporary furniture accented by several full-size floor plants. I could smell the 'come-hither' odors of dinner being prepared in their kitchen which was in the center of the first floor. Luther showed me into the dining room where I assumed possessed Althea's stamp of colors—chocolate brown walls having a slight sheen in between the stark white painted molding.

I sat down on one of the chairs on the longest side of the dining table while Luther sat at the end of the table closest to me. The woman of the house appeared at the kitchen archway looking stunning and very tall in a flowing purple blouse and matching dress pants. "Glenda, I'm glad you came. Do you want white or red wine? I'm serving a roast pork which can go either way."

"I would like white, thanks."

"Glenda, you look ragged, all drawn in the face." Luther observed.

"We got a break today, but it was pretty touch and go. Wyla and I went back to the Rathbone's only with not an invitation." I said, taking my wine glass from Althea.

I turned to Luther. I said with a wink. "Oh, by the way, throughout the search in that tower. I did not see or hear one cat."

I did not get a chance to further divulge what the break in the case was, Althea had brought in our entire three-course meal on a giant ceramic platter. She put the platter in the center of the table. "Now, you two, don't be shy. I did Luther's job of carving the roast in the kitchen. Serve yourselves, I'm no servant!"

"Well, I can tell you both this. The FBI agent and I broke into the Rathbone place and I was able to get some vital evidence in The Tower. I'm praying. I won't hear all shit hit the fan from my sergeant." I continued, while spooning the carrots, potatoes, celery next to my slices of roast pork smothered in brown gravy.

Althea said. "I don't know if you will get a balling out from your sergeant. He came to see me at the hospital."

Luther added. "My outspoken lady told him every gory detail of her attacker. Mitch got up, bent over and kissed her forehead like he was her father."

"Glenda, with Althea you have a solid confession from a professional in the mental health profession. And we have a trip coming up which will give this bizarre case more tooth." Luther said, taking in some of his dinner.

All of us went about consuming our delicious and savory dinner before Althea scolded us for letting it get cold. Through the dinner and on into drinking more wine, I forgot about bringing my news to the table talk. Althea dropped a curious tidbit of information to me.

"Luther and I are going to Algiers with a flight to New Orleans in the morning out of Indianapolis International."

"Why Algiers? I assume, this is not a pleasure vacation. Algiers is known to be quite dangerous." I said, putting down my wine glass.

"Well, it is about who we are to see not what we want to see. There is a shaman there who has agreed to see us." Luther said, then stared at me seeing I looked totally clueless. "A shaman has healing powers, known to interact with the spirits. Her name is Luana Barba, she is Filipina, originally from Roxas City in the Philippines."

I sat there almost on the verge of tears. A rarity for this type of bubbling emotion was from complete exhaustion and the fact Luther was still in the game. I had not been a fan of Althea, but tonight she seemed so different. She became another believer to the small group forming who was willing to take on an unknown evil that all of us would not stop the gruesome violence until we became like that shaman in Algiers.

Chapter Eleven

Dangerous Mind

Romeo Blanco took the time on a Monday while the restaurant was closed to make some orders for the more specialty dishes. His office door was opened, so he had no trouble in hearing the pounding on the kitchen door. The bartender heard it also. He made it to the door before Romeo.

There was a petite beautiful Filipina proud in her shiny long wavy black hair dressed in fancy evening clothes on the other side of the door. This time she wasn't wearing sunglasses, her amber eyes were dancing, her full mouth formed into a pleasing smile.

"Good evening, is Romeo here?"

The bartender Ling said, "Why, yes. I'll get him."

"Don't bother, Ling. I heard the lady ask for me. I'll take it from here." Romeo said, walking around from behind Ling, a most obedient Asian type gentleman who possessed a highly precise way of carrying himself which made him an asset to Blanco.

"Well, well, the lady herself! I was expecting a curt email when I told you I couldn't provide the balut anymore." Romeo said, getting closer to her as she walked inside the center of the kitchen.

Amora Rathbone raised her thin ladylike fingers to stroke his chest hair—peeking out from his V-necked Polo shirt. "My Romeo, I harbor no hard feelings. I know you received a visit from a couple of detectives. I was more disappointed I would not get to see your handsome face again."

"Wow! I wasn't expecting for you to be so generous." Romeo gasped, getting turned on by her sudden affection.

"Tell you what. I've made a reservation at The Drake's dining room. Let's say, I want to smoke the peace pipe in the form of a high-caloric high-class dinner for two. I'm sure, you'll appreciate the special menu the dining room has been famous for." Amora said, almost with a purring sound to her soft voice.

"Well, I can't turn that down. Let me change into more appropriate dress in my office. Won't be long." Romeo heartily agreed.

Amora and Romeo were taken to the famous Chicago hotel by the Rathbone butler, Wesley Thornton. Throughout the forty-minute drive Wesley could hear the groaning and moaning of sexual body-banter in the backseat. Pulling into the front entrance of The Drake Hotel, he used a discretionary period of time before he opened the back door of the sleek black limousine.

The well-dressed attractive and sexually-charged couple rolled out of the backseat made their way to the entrance. The couple during the dining process of feeding each other oysters-on-the-halfshell, drinking large amounts of a California red blend vintage along with consuming respective entrees of prime rib went about a post-sexual exchange.

They came outside of the hotel entrance to notice the night air was uncomfortably still. Another summer heat wave had hit the Midwest. Wesley Thorton dutifully pulled up performing his poised routine—stop, get out, and make sure the couple got into the backseat safely. Amora looked up and whispered to Wesley. "Drive to a Milwaukee dense wooded area, first exit. Take it."

Romeo's motor was running on a high caliber of sexual arousal. Amora sat there willing for him to begin the dance again. Her full supple lips felt like velvet. Something wicked brewed as Romeo began to realize Amora's petite soft body to transform.

Her hair disappeared into a rough bald head full of warts. The softness of her lips changed to a feeling of scales where her teeth partially decayed smelled of death. The remaining teeth became sharp razor-like fangs, tearing away his clothes to get to his flesh in his midsection.

Wesley kept driving, pushing a button for a divider to muffle the inhuman sounds of savagery, as well as shield the reflection from the rearview mirror of a man being eaten, still in the state of consciousness. It is unconscionable that a highly efficient cultured man could let this type of killing go on without stopping it.

The butler held his terror in check, knowing full well the beast Amora transformed into could sense his revulsion combined with hot fear. He pulled into an exit for The Tupelo Wilderness—travelling deep into a dense woods away from any passing traffic.

Wesley moved in trepidation, looking down as Amora used her wing-span to scoop out the torn body of Romeo Blanco. The butler took out cleaning cloths and a bucket of solutions. Wiping and drying the entire backseat gave Amora the time to dump the body and transform back to her human shape.

Putting the cleaning bucket, trash bag of soiled cloths, Wesley pulled out a small piece of luggage. He shut the truck, simultaneous action to hand Amora her bag, then opening the back door for her. During the heinous evening of sexual liaison, high-class dinner, and post-meal of human aspic, Wesley stayed in his dutiful role of a trusted servant.

I was able to bed down early, knowing Luther might be coming back into the fold of law enforcement. In a dream state during my rem sleep, I became a watcher in a step-by-step progression of a highly unusual night of combining food consumption with cold-blooded murder.

The couple I watched were suspended above some ethereal canopy. The exchanged behavior was intense in their shared hunger for sexual pleasure. They moved on to an elegantly-set table fit for the very rich. After dinner, they moved on in the backseat of a moving vehicle to resume more sexual play.

Suddenly being plagued by loud ticking, blood-curdling cries from a man in the throes of unbelievable fear and agony caused me to jerk and thrash all over my bed. The next image I saw and actually felt—the victim's midsection almost torn in two with his pancreas and liver eaten away. The shock of my body falling to the wood floor woke me from my tortured night visions.

Like a shot hit me, I got up and ran to the bathroom. I doused my head in the sink with cold water as if the shock of the coldness could vanquish those horrific images. Going back to sleep was impossible. My mouth was so dry, it was hard to swallow.

I went to the liquor cabinet, pouring whiskey halfway into a short glass. Something strong on my tongue helped to keep me from screaming.

I went into my kitchen, and chased the whiskey with a glass of ice water before making a pot of coffee. Drinking the strongest coffee I could make, I sat down at my dining table and went into a childhood pastime of sketching.

As dawn approached, I had filled four pages with images. One of the pages revealed the face of the victim. His round dark eyes were filled with an intense amount of fear with his mouth opened—as if he was crying out in sheer agony for his life.

I studied the shape of his nose, his specific structure of his square-shaped cheeks and strong manly chin. I shouted out in the solitude of my quiet apartment. "This is that restaurant manager, Romeo Blanco!"

The other images drawn as a series of revealing sketches of the dramatic transformation—no white hair from what I had previously seen. The head of the transforming creature was bald with several ugly warts. Its teeth looked to be varied, some rotted, others to be razor sharp. The bat like wings visible, taking up the torn victim to a remote place for disposal.

My next mode of action—get Agent Stark to see these sketches. John, Paul, and George would tout off, saying all those revealing images were mute due to showing up in a dream. Over the last three months, my sarcasm about this legend had changed to fully embracing every aspect of it down to supernatural auspices affecting my very dream state.

Chapter Twelve

Luana Barba

After setting into their hotel accommodations in downtown New Orleans, Luther and Althea took a short ferry ride from the foot of Canal Street to Algiers Port. Among the shops and restaurants was a small corner house made in concrete block and stucco. A tattered sign hung above a corner storefront read, "Luana's Herbs and Divinities."

Althea was attracted to a large glass cabinet in the store containing an array of ceramic figurines dressed in ornate dress with fancy headdresses looking like halos. A brown skinned young girl looked to be fifteen came out of a red velvet curtain.

She leaned on the top counter of the long glass cabinet where Althea raised up quickly to meet her face. "Oh, you caught me admiring the many figurines you have here. What are they?"

"They are called Divinities, each one is a saint like St. Lucy, St. Katherine and so on. Many people buy them to decorate their homes, or these saints give them a strong feeling of godly protection." The young girl explained with a noticeable accent.

Luther made his way to join his wife. "Hello, Miss. Is there a Luana Barba here?"

The teenager compiled due to Luther's subtle authoritative way. She said, "Yes, I will get her. Can I have your name?"

"Yes, we are Luther and Althea from Indiana."

A shorter woman somewhat wrinkled on her face and neck came out from the curtain. Her almond-shaped dark eyes penetrated as she greeted them. "You two are the Midwesterners I spoke to via email over the last two weeks. Yes?"

"Yes, we came to Algiers specifically to talk to you about aswang." Althea said.

Luana made jerky movements with her neck and hands, conveying to them that type of utterance might make the other customers quite nervous, even enough to flee. "Join me behind this curtain. Now, the both of you!"

They followed the small woman to a spacious backroom—combination sitting room and kitchen possessing a different look, run down not modern like the front room.

"You folks sit over there at the round table. I will be there to join you after I mix these herbs for a customer coming in soon." Luana instructed.

Luana brought over a glass bottle the size of a medium salt shaker filled with a creamy liquid. Luther began their interview with a question. "Why is a shaman important where an aswang infiltrates a place?"

"Shamans are able to speak to spirit guides, and sometimes they act as mediums during pag-anite séance rituals. In modern times Filipino society you can see these shamans as folk healers, apothecaries about to address ailments like I do here."

"Luana, you have my complete experience on one of the emails I sent. What are you able to do for me? Daily I'm plagued with the aftermath of what that creature did to me." Althea said with tears in her eyes.

Luana took Althea's hands, she softly said. "With the both of you clearing your minds of any Western Christian doctrine, I can communicate to a spirit guide. He or she will entreat for a healing."

"Can you also give me a way to fight this evil?" Luther spoke up.

Luana got up, then turned off every overhead light. This backroom possessed no windows. There was only a small crack of subdued light from where the curtains met. She brought over a thick cylinder-shaped white lighted candle and placed it in the center of the table.

"Wrap your hands into each other's arms. Concentrate on my every utterance with your eyes opened." Luana told them.

She began chanting in a language they didn't recognize. She sat silent for a few minutes—a pink light covered her face and neck. As she raised her voice speaking against some sort of unfriendly entity her face turned blood red.

Luther and Althea looked at each other with their eyes wide and full of terror. Luana called out a name five times. She clapped. She got up, then turned the lights back on. She came back to the table and took Althea's hands again in hers.

"My fearful one, the creature who attacked you will not come back to you. For one reason, Althea, you fought back. This aswang left your city for a more Northern country. The only way if aswang comes back to your city if there is a family concern."

Luther asked, confused. "What do you mean by a family concern?"

"This one comes from a powerful family in Indiana. Her connection will make her become compromised. If matters get to a place where Detective Charles, you have to go against her. I have something for you." Luana passed him the bottle she sat down with. "What is in this jar, a mixture of ground mandrake root and bull semen will render her powerless for a short time. I stress only a short time."

Althea spoke up. "Luther and his partner will want to pressure the law enforcement envelope to take the creature in rather than kill it."

"If that is the case. The aswang needs to be strung up from a high place, and beat from the back many times until it spews out what we call, 'the chick'." Luana said, handing the jar to Luther.

On the plane trip back to Indianapolis International Airport, both Luther and Althea were dumbfounded on their findings from Luana. Over two white wines, Luther told his fiancé, "Imagine me and Glenda veteran police who have been trained for zero tolerance on police brutality to volunteer to beat a suspect almost to death until they cough up some kind of fantasy chick living in their body since adolescence."

Althea took Luther's hand. She squeezed it as she began to scold him. "Baby, I once was a skeptic to all of this supernatural business. When that little brown woman took ahold of my hands, I felt a powerful surge of wellbeing. We better heed to what she told us."

Chapter Thirteen

Trip To Milwaukee

I got to work rushing to Wyla's desk to share my vivid night terrors. "You have got to hear this!" Wyla got up from her seat, put her hand up to stop me from talking.

She said as she put on her jacket. "Save it until I get back in a few days. I've got a lead from my top brass to travel up to Wisconsin with the Beatle guys. We are leaving now."

I was left feeling clueless and somewhat embarrassed to be pushed aside in such an abrupt way. All the weeks of my hard work compiling clues and facts to share with Wyla, and the generosity to bring her and the other agents in, caused me to feel like the odd-man out.

I stormed into Mitch Gable's office—no knock, no apology for my sudden intrusion. "Sarg, what the hell? Why wasn't I included to go up north with them?"

He peaked over his black framed reading glasses, "I guess you deserve an explanation. Sit down, and don't interrupt until I'm finished!"

"Glenda, you have an amazing nose for evidence. You're one of the best detectives here in the division along with Charles. Both of you can handle the victims to a place they trust giving you details no matter how difficult. My dear, you are unraveling week by week. I had a conversation with your partner Luther this morning. He's coming in from Algiers with Althea later this afternoon. I'll give you the flight info. Meet them at the airport." Gable talked to me in such a way, I could not argue.

Luther and Althea gave over smiles and shouts when they spied me coming toward them at the baggage claim. Luther said before I opened my mouth. "Follow us to the first exit for an Applebee's off of I465 East."

No questions, I carefully followed a smooth transition to their destination on Allisonville Road. For the first time since Althea's horrific attack, she took me by the arm and showed me a gracious touch of affection between us. I was a little bit suspicious of her changed behavior towards me, but part of me was delighted.

We took a booth in the back part of the restaurant where there was plenty of privacy. Althea, true to her condition ordered a full course entrée while Luther and I went light for the house salad.

"I'm all ears. How did the Barba woman give both of you such evident turn-around of the high hopes I witness now?" I probed.

Athea shared first. "This trip was a great idea. Luana reassured me through this eerie séance, this creature was in no way interested in coming after me again."

"Glenda, she went through a process of speaking to a spirit guide who came forth with information you had obtained about her father, and what would bring her back to Anderson." Luther interjected.

"You keep saying, "her". Are you referring to Amora Rathbone?" I pressed.

"Luana kept referring to the aswang in the female gender during the entire time we talked to her."

I leaned back, then shook my head. "Well, that blows the theory of Wyla saying the assailant is Amado Rathbone."

"He is probably protecting her, as is Evan Rathbone and the butler. This family will do anything, lie over and over to protect her."

"Don't leave out what Luana is sending us in the mail, Luther." Althea said as she began eating her grilled salmon.

"Oh, that's what will help us bring her in. This jar of mandrake root and bull semen will leave her powerless. We've got to make sure she gets doused with it in the face. The hard part is getting to string her up, with those enormous wings. You and I taking care of this impossible task won't be enough." Luther said.

I shouted in full blown excitement. "Whoa, Luther! Sounds like you're getting back into the case!"

"When we talked to Mitch on the phone, he told me about the agents going up to Milwaukee on a lead about a savage murder. Glenda, we can get the details from technology, and continue on with the victim list." Luther said, sounding like he had not been away at all.

"So, you know without what's on paper that the lead of this murder could have Amora's stamp of ghoulish behavior. I don't have all the facts yet, but I feel the connection to our victim list." I said, giving Luther my squinty-eye look.

"You should have been there. This small brown Filipina lady took Athea and I into a spiritual Intel where she was told about Amora's next move. We were freaking out but both of us were getting her expertise needed to be noted." Luther said, staying on the breakthrough from the Algiers' trip.

Wyla Stark and the other three agents walked into the Milwaukee Police Department first landing at the front desk. Wyla flashed her badge at the tall heavy-set black policewoman.

"Officer, we are FBI from the Chicago office, affiliated with Anderson PD in Indiana, station sergeant, Mitch Gable. Could we speak with Detective Mason Doyle?"

The officer showed complete understanding. "By all means, Detective Doyle's office is through here to the third door to the left. You can come on through." She said, then pressed a button underneath the high counter.

The agent, Wyla called John knocked on the open door molding. "We're the FBI agents coming in from the Anderson PD."

The large bulky blonde headed detective got up from looking through a file. "Come on in. Grab a seat if there's enough."

Wyla took one seat in front of the detective's desk while John sat beside her. The other two agents stood to the right of where Detective Doyle was seated. Detective Doyle began the conversation. "Well, the victim had been in the woods for a few days, any face ID was impossible. The body was a bloody hamburger mess. The only thing I recognized were his fancy Italian shoes."

"Funny you would notice the shoes after the body was such a mess. Why did that stick out to you?" Wyla began the questions.

"Well, agent, this gives me an idea the man was well-to-do. When we get a lead like that, the brand and what stores carry them will lead us to the identification. There was no wallet or any other kind of way to ID him except for what we find out with the autopsy." Detective Doyle said.

"Well, I guess, that's our next step to go to where the autopsy is." Wyla said, getting up from her chair.

"All of you can squeeze into my SUV out back in the department parking lot."

Forensics had the victim laid out in the basement of Milwaukee General. The group came as the director of forensics had begun the procedure. Agent Wyla looked over at the agent she called, "Paul". He was noticeably gagging as he looked at the torn up body of the victim.

"The liver and the pancreas were completely devoured. Strange, the victim's genitals are void of any blood with an inkling of complete engorged tissues deflated from some kind of strong suction." The director explained as he took a probe to point out the precise location. The agent Wyla called "George" wrote down every word in his iPad.

"Paul, looks like you've seen and heard enough." Wyla said. She thought to herself, *I can take the condition of the victim but if Paul pukes in front of me. I will lose my breakfast.* She turned to Detective Doyle. "Where are his shoes?"

The director spoke up. "Agent, I have bagged them. You can have a look, they are over there. I must insist all of you wear gloves as you examine them."

All four agents walked over to a white marbled counter to the right of the double stainless steel sinks. Wyla carefully pulled out the shoes caked with dried dirt and dead insects. Her reference point of Italian brand men's shoes was zero. While John came forward showing by his alarmed face he knew the brand.

"Wow! I haven't seen these kind of shoes since I was in Rome two years ago. These are a pair of Alessandro Demesure leather oxfords. This man was either well off or they were a gift. They run a little over $2,000!"

"George, put your iPad to work and find out any stores that carry the brand." Wyla suggested, turning behind her.

Waiting for George's search, Wyla stepped out of the autopsy room to use her cell phone. "Hey, Glen, you're not still pissed at me?"

I made an audible huff over the connection, then said. "Well, you caught me off guard. I had something to show you. Well, I guess. I'm cool. What's up?"

"Well, the victim this time is a male. Seems to be some sort of individual who buys 2,000-dollar Italian dress shoes. He was really a mess. If this is the same suspect we've been pursuing, they changed their MO by devouring inner organs." Wyla told me.

"Remember, Althea had part of her liver torn into and devoured. Seems to me, this assailant is either trying to trick us or she is getting more violent." I said, bringing forth a decisive turn to the case.

I thought of a question. "Hey, Wyla, could you tell the color and texture of the man's hair?"

"How astute of you, and not viewing the condition of the body. At first glance, the hair was matted up with dirt and dried leaves mixed with black-looking blood. With gloved fingers, I felt around. The hair was wavy, coarse and seemed to be dark brown."

"How about the torn clothing that was left on his body?" I asked.

"You're scaring me with this *Sherlock Holmes* line of deductions. The left over clothes have been bagged. We will give them a solid study. I'll get back. Later." Wyla said, then clicked off.

I thought with my last question, Wyla was confused about why I would ask such detailed probing about what the victim was wearing. These last few weeks working with her, I realized she prefers to come up with her own conclusions on the details of our ongoing pursuit. I might have tugged at her being uncomfortable with my new self-reliant probes—ones identified to her as an oversight in detection.

Spending a relaxing evening in my apartment that night after I spoke to Wyla, I realized the knowledge Luther was back in full regalia of his infamous investigative prowess gave me the opportunity to sleep sound for the first time in weeks. Before my heavy lids blinked for the last time, I knew Luther would jump on the chance to travel up north to Downers Grove.

Chapter Fourteen
Enough Killing

Amora came downstairs for a rare occasion of spending breakfast with her father. "My dear, you look absolutely transformed!" Ethan Rathbone gasped with an alarmed expression.

She threw back her straight black hair then reached for a small bowl resembling a dark red aspic. She laughed, spoke through her apparent frivolity. "I took a break from my usual fare to partake of a human type of sweetbreads."

Her father winced in a sudden repulsion. He knew the hidden meaning of that bragging statement to be something unconscionable to imagine. He put up his right hand like a road cop stopping a vehicle in downtown city traffic. "Amora, you know how I abhor your secret words that only Wesley and I can translate."

"Father, you asked. I thought you would be used to my lot in life by now."

Ethan clapped as if to magically erase his queasy stomach by his hands making that loud repetitive sound. "Change of subject. Let's talk about Divinia. Any progress?"

"I'm going in today to test it?"

"I hope you aren't going to use yourself as the guinea pig! Let's not entertain the same action from the horror classic, *Dr. Jeykell & Mr. Hyde.*"

"Father, time is of the essence. *Hyde* comes to the fore more often than I like. The list is getting longer, and those law enforcement ladies are not going to go away!" Amora said. She ate the dark red jellied substance, and slithered up from the table.

As she walked out of the formal dining room, Ethan Rathbone buried his head in his hands. In a jerk of his neck, he shouted out, "Wesley, I need you in the dining room!"

Wesley possessed a monitoring device he had placed very close to him in the kitchen. In matter of minutes, he showed up at Ethan's side at the head of the dining table. "What's you need, Sir?"

"I've had a belly full of these non-ending killings. Get ahold of Luana Barba. Make sure you tell her this is for the process of annihilation. Otherwise, she will hang up on you. I can't go on like this!" Ethan told the butler, then went into a state of complete sobs. A display of hopelessness Wesley had not seen before.

Amora stood by the stone staircase. She possessed a gift of long range hearing. She had heard every word her father uttered. The staircase was located many feet from the main foyer where the dining room was located at the right side of the massive estate. Not totally without feeling, as she listened, a line of tears rolled down her left cheek.

Wesley did not waste any time in contacting Luana Barba. She knew his name very well. She said nothing only breathed heavily in the long distance connection. "Luana, don't hang up. This call is to solicit your help for the total end of Amora Rathbone. Master Ethan and I have been party to her attacks for years since adolescence. Now, Ethan found out from this morning's breakfast conversation, she has gone onto a form of ghoulish behavior."

She asked a pertinent question. "Are you and Mr. Rathbone sure her finality has to be? What you want will take effort."

"From what was brought forth this morning, she acted rather cavalier. She admitted to going under dosage tests herself for this new drug she has developed, Divinia. We both believe her behavior is not improving but getting much worse. In the past, Amora showed so much pathos and sorrow. She would spend days in one of the more empty rooms in the upper level of the Tower after some of her killings. I thought it was because she destroyed babies, so I would leave her alone."

"All right, you are to send me a parcel of the developing drug, Divinia. It will take some research on my part to find the proper lethal mixture to stop her heart. In a timely manner before the sun comes up, you are to dismember her then incinerate the body parts. This will take a strong reserve." Luana instructed.

"I believe, all the leg work will depend on me. Master Ethan has suffered so much anguish for years. I will do anything to give him peace." The butler said, reassuring the shaman all her instructions would be followed.

For years, Wesley was aware the many magical powers Amora had been given as this curse came into maturity. She could read fear in someone by visualizing their eyes and feeling the acceleration of their breathing many feet away from them.

He made a search of her Tower quarters to find a bottle of Divinia in her bathroom. He looked at the number prescribed, then counted the pills left in the bottle—only two taken. He decided to make a trip to the Saxony facility to pay a friendly visit to Amora's secretary.

The secretary an attractive middle-age woman with shining blue eyes held a noticeable crush on Wesley. He walked in, dressed in a gray suit that accentuated his blue eyes. "Clarissa, is Miss Amora in?"

"No, Wesley. She's in a meeting at the main office." Clarissa told him, smiling and leaning in where he sat on her desk.

Wesley took her hand. "I'm in a dilemma here. Our gardener was caught pilfering the last of her Divinia prescription. Could you get me a refill, so her monthly dosage will not be interrupted?"

"Yes, but shouldn't we wait until I let Amora know what has happened?"

"Clarissa, you well know any hiccup in Amora's routine can send her into a seizure." Wesley said softly, stroking her hand.

The secretary let forth a heavy sigh, then picked up the phone. After hanging up, she said. "One of the research assistants will bring it to this office in a few minutes."

Wesley smiled, and laid on the charm thicker. "Well, gorgeous, let's talk about where I'll be taking you to dinner."

After he had the bottle in hand, and promised to pick up Clarissa at 6—every move was orchestrated. He evened out the bottle in Amora's bathroom. Drove off to the closest post office to send the parcel to Luana "Overnight Delivery". He was able to get the night off from Ethan to make his dinner date. He used the secretary, but he thought a dinner with someone who adored his company was an adequate trade-off.

Chapter Fifteen

A Parking Lot Visitation

Late in the evening after saying my good-nights to Wyla and Luther, I looked forward to my comfy apartment. Maybe watch something good from my DVD collection, or I could curl up with a good book. I unlocked my vehicle, turned my head hearing my name from a man's voice.

"It's been awhile, but I knew you would be getting off work." Amado Rathbone came out of the fog from an all-day drowning of rain.

I jerked back. His sudden appearance gave me a jolted fright. I wasn't sure how to take him standing in front of me. "My God, Amado! I would have preferred a phone call instead of this late night creep in the department parking lot."

"I realize this seems impulsive. At work today I couldn't stop thinking about you. Could we go somewhere and talk?" He asked, slowly getting closer to me. I stared into those alluring amber eyes of his.

"The only place I know that is open Unc's White Corner. You and I ran into each other there once." I said.

The place at 11:30 p.m. was fairly wiped out. We took a booth in a corner of the front dining area. I was not altogether comfortable being with him at such a late hour in a place almost empty. I wanted us to sit where the one tending bar could see us. I squirmed when Amado sat in the same side of the booth, eye to eye, shoulder to shoulder.

Unc's youngest son approached our table. "Wow! Late night, Glenda? What can I get for you two?"

"Do you have Chivas?" Amado asked.

"Yes, we do."

"I'll take a double with a glass of ice water."

I ordered. "Get me my usual on draft."

"Now, why did you show up at this late hour? I didn't swallow the 'thinking of me all day' thing." I acted cagey.

"These last few days my father is quite concerned with my sister. Your insisting on suspecting her has forced her to go through dangerous testing of the Divinia drug on herself. The drug is not altogether ready for humans." Amado told me, his eyes staring so intense I sat there frozen, not able to look away.

His penetrating stare with those alluring amber eyes made me forget he had cast a spell on me when Wyla and I saw him in his father's office at the Rathbone estate. I felt helpless. I managed to go on with a semblance of conversation, hoping he would stop staring.

"Well, I thought the drug was ready to be launched from the first meeting we had three months ago."

Our drinks came. We stopped while Amado threw back his drink in one gulp. I sat there and nursed my beer. I wanted so much to touch him, to kiss him. There was a strong compulsion for me to throw myself at him. I struggled to hold back, so I took another few sips of my mug.

I put my hand on his right arm. My guard came down to demonstrate a concern for his welfare. "Amado, you seem intensely disturbed. What's troubling you? For some strange reason, I want to help."

Amado answered me with an alarming embrace, kissing me over and over. I hadn't been kissed like that in years. It was a feeling of falling into a deep swoon with my eyes wide open. I wanted more, and I didn't care how bad it would be if I got totally caught up with him. Wyla didn't trust him, enough so—she was convinced he was the guilty one who was our special person of interest. I traveled back to the night when he first kissed me, and I wanted him to make love to me in the worst way.

Drinking the rest of my beer in two more gulps, we left a twenty on the table. In what seemed like seconds Amado and I were groping each other on my front room couch. In between kisses, I threw my clothes all over the couch and carpet. Unable to move, or not wanting to protest, Amado systematically in intense sensations proceeded to pleasure me with his fingers and his mouth.

What I remembered next, I was opening my eyes to the strong sunlight coming in from the double windows in the dining room nook off of my kitchen. Coming out of my cocoon wrapping of a multi-colored throw Grandpa Pete gave me at Christmas last year, I realized I was naked and left to sleep overnight on my couch.

I managed to gather myself enough to cover up in my purple Turkish bathrobe from the bathroom. My mouth was foul for some strange reason. I got to the kitchen thinking a cup of the strongest coffee could erase the bad taste in my mouth. Not able to make coffee, I heard a loud pounding on my door. I picked up my phone—time, 12:30 p.m., two texts from Luther and the incessant pounding didn't stop.

I opened the door, and saw an annoyed Luther. "You look like shit! I've sent two texts." He sailed past me, and made himself at home making me a pot of coffee. I realized as I closed my door, I had a nasty headache. I took two Tylenols with a glass of water. Standing next to Luther, thinking *'Did Amado happen or did I have one huge wet dream after a draft at Unc's?'*

I took the time to read Luther's texts, *"Partner, let's get shaking here!"* One message. The next message was more insistent. *"We've got the road trip to do. Glenda, call me back, ASAP!"*

"Sit down, sleeping beauty and drink the coffee I made." Luther said, leading me to the dining room table. I took three sips and began to feel like I was conscious. Luther waved at me, insistent I look at him, "We've got another victim. It was called in while you slept the morning away!"

"My God, here, I'm trying to wrap my head around what the hell happened last night. Seriously, another victim, this is getting ridiculous!"

I took my coffee, and pointed at Luther. "I'm getting a shower and will be with you ASAP."

During the shower and getting my pantsuit on with the usual routine of shoulder holster, checking my gun and putting my wallet in my left hand pant pocket my mind was full of jumbled images. *Amado kissing me on the couch, then taking off my shirt, bra, then massaging various parts of my body waist-up. The images continued for me, seeing him fully clothed walking to my front door. He did happen, but why do I feel so strange and so ashamed?*

I walked out of my bedroom, and asked Luther a question. "What day is it?"

"Partner, what the hell is with you. It's Tuesday. Looks like you lost a day. I called and texted you yesterday off and on, got nothing."

"I think I know why I lost a day, but after we find out about this new victim. I don't think you are going to like me very much when I tell you." I said, almost ready to confess about Amado.

During the drive to Shadyside Recreation Park, Luther pressed me to tell him. "You know, let's get this over with. Spill it!"

"All right, Sunday night I went into the division to go over all the details of the chart we made. I was there until late, about 11:30 p.m. Amado Rathbone met me in the APD parking lot. We had a drink at Unc's and as far as it seems we were with each other. I'm not sure when he left. It's all a blur, because I slept like I have not done before. Like I was drugged." I sat there as Luther listened. He didn't look at me, shook his head and grunted.

He pulled into a driveway on a slight incline from busy Cross St., very close to one of the park's entrances. We parked behind a 2010 rented silver Honda Civic. Wyla Stark met us at the front door. She held it open for us. "I hope you two haven't eaten lunch. She's hamburger from the waist down."

I looked at the victim's face, then my eyes moved down. This job had desensitized me to torn up bodies and massive spillage of blood, but there was one factor caused me to almost lose it in front of everyone milling around. I knew the victim. Her matted bloodied blonde hair and her open dead eyes a faded color of green. It was Katie Fisher, the waitress from The Bobber's Café.

Examining her lower extremities, I said to myself, '*He kept me busy while his sister butchered Katie*'. I began to shake uncontrollably, my arms and my lower jaw quivered with every word the coroner was saying to Luther who was behind us both.

Wyla pulled me away from the gory bathroom scene. "Girl, you've got to get yourself together. Seems to me you're unraveling bit by bit with this case. These navy blues will have a field day crucifying your ass since that chart in the division is the talk of the whole APD building."

Wyla was right, in seventeen years of police work this is the first time I showed any kind of weakness. I took in some cleansing breaths to calm my nerves. Luther came out to the living room to join us. He suggested we all three get out of there, and take a breather at The Toast.

This type of downtown diner had been an established throwback to the hamburger joints in the 1950s and 1960s. It was not too far from our detective division. We ordered all coffees to go around. I thought maybe a bowl of vegetable soup would be good for me. Wyla sat scratched her head and ordered the famous Toast double cheeseburger platter.

When my soup got placed in front of me, I made a mad dash to the ladies bathroom. I threw up in the savior of a toilet bowl. Washing and drying my face, I felt somewhat recovered. I went back to the table, Luther and Wyla were discussing something. I sat down they stopped talking.

Luther turned to me in the booth where all of us had a view to the busy daily downtown traffic on Main Street. "I told Wyla all that transpired in Algiers with the shaman yesterday."

"It seems to me this assailant is getting hungry for human flesh going in for the inner organs. In the beginning of the case, there were only attacks to the pregnant women to get to their babies. There seems to be a change in the assailant's mode of lifestyle where the dead babies is not enough." Wyla said.

"You know if anyone was sitting close to us with you saying all that gore, they would either lose their lunch or get up and leave." I told her, holding my stomach.

"Glenda, you're losing your edge." Wyla surmised by my queasiness.

"She's having some regrets about how she spent Sunday night." Luther said.

There it was. I had to spill my guts about my mysterious indiscretion. I was not only still feeling sick, but added to it was total embarrassment on letting Amado have his way with me.

"All right, you might as well know it, too. I spent some romantic time with Amado very late. Now, I'm having all the regrets, embarrassment, and seeing Katie really tipped the scales for me." I confessed.

"That explains your behavior at the scene. Shame on you for sleeping with the enemy." Wyla said, her eyes read she was furious with me and her body language showed her complete disgust.

"I've got to say you guys can crucify me all you want. I think as this day progresses, Amado used some type of magic or hypnosis on me to get me to let down my guard. I know how damaging it is to get too close to someone we might be looking to as a suspect. I'm convinced he kept me busy while his sister did the deed on Katie." I said, getting louder with each word.

"Calm down, Glenda. Wyla and I came to the conclusion to make the trip up to Downers Grove which could very well tie what she learned in Milwaukee to Katie's murder. Stop lamenting and eat your soup." Luther said, stopping me like he knew how to.

Chapter Sixteen

The Restaurant

All three of us caffeine-fueled officers of the law left The Toast and made our way for a four-hour road trip. By the time we arrived at The Singapore Sling, Ling met us at the front counter with a puzzled expression.

"Officers, are you here about the disappearance of Mr. Blanco?"

Luther told him. "Yes, Ling, hoping you can help us. Is there someone who can take over for you while we ask some questions of you?"

Ling nodded, then snapped his fingers. An Asian woman fairly young dressed in a close-fitting red gold ornamental dress much like Chinese women would wear in a formal way came forward. He whispered to her.

"Officers, follow me to the back of the restaurant past the kitchen. Mr. Blanco had an office there." Ling said.

Wyla spoke when we reached a part of the office away from the ears of the kitchen. She used no sensitivity in getting Ling prepared for what he was about to hear. "Ling, your manager has been murdered. His body was found last week in a wooded area outside of Milwaukee."

Ling rocked back and forth almost as if he was going to faint. He sat down at Blanco's office desk chair. His breathing accelerated, he was on the verge of hysterics. I thought to get him some water. There was a water cooler next to a couple of tall file cabinets. As I was filling up a paper cup with cold water I looked up.

My eyes glanced at a hanging camera device hooked to a corner molding close to the filing cabinets. I gave Ling the cup of water. All of us stood over him like a mother hovering over an upset child.

"Is there something you can tell us?" Wyla probed, forcing Ling to answer.

"What do you mean?" Ling asked, still confused.

I put my hand on Ling's shoulder. "Ling, what Agent Stark means was there any kind of visitor for Mr. Blanco recently?"

He looked in deep thought, then jerked and looked up at us. "Two weeks ago, one of his clients who regularly purchased the balut came in from the back door. She seemed to be there to talk to Mr. Blanco." Ling told us.

What did the woman look like?" Wyla asked.

"It was the pretty Filipina woman from Indiana. Mr. Blanco told me to go back to the front while he talked to her."

"Ling, is there a way we can view a history of who comes into this area and leaves?" I asked.

"Yes, every month I am to store the cartridge from the camera transfer it to a file on the computer. My recent file I created a month ago." Ling said.

Luther asked. "Could you bring up the file, so we could view it?"

Ling nodded a positive response and went through the motions on the desk PC to open up the file. What we saw at first was kitchen help coming and going, then halfway through scrolling down there was Romeo Blanco opening the back door for Amora Rathbone. The date on the corner of the screen to be two weeks ago on a Monday, the first week of September.

Luther asked Ling. "Why was Blanco in the back room at this particular time and day?"

Ling turned around and looked up at Luther. "Sir, we are closed on Mondays. That is when Mr. Blanco does inventory and paperwork. I usually help him with the inventory."

Wyla bent down, penetrating an authoritative stare at Ling. "Can you transfer this to a flash drive so we can use this evidence for our case?"

"Oh, Yes, I will be glad to. Anything to find out who killed Mr. Blanco. He was not only good to me as a boss but has helped me several times with my yearly Visas." Ling said. Luther wrote out on a blank sheet of copy paper the address of the detective division in Anderson and attached his business card.

Luther on the dark interstate going south on I65 brought up an intriguing and bizarre premise. "Ladies, imagine tying all these victims to what we believe came from a centuries-old aswang who comes from the sky to attack or kill them to overcome some burning curse. Can you actually think the city prosecutor can prove this in our modern-times court?"

"I'm trying to wrap my head around how to give my superior at the agency the most recent update. We've had some bizarre cases, but usually the suspect was classified as a serious psychopath not someone who could turn into an evil flying creature." Wyla said, shrugging her shoulders.

I chimed in. "We are going to tell all that we have, no matter how strange. It will land how it does. Knowing human nature, we might be forced to call the killer out. I don't know how many more torn up victims I can look at!"

What I said must have brought to the surface an inkling Wyla actually possessed some kind of a heart. She looked at me, lowering her eyelids and took my arm. I translated that as she fully understood how I was felt seeing Katie being all torn up.

We got back to the division. Mitch was still in his office. From his open door, he whistled, motioning for us to get into his inner sanctum. We filed in, Wyla, Luther, and I.

The sergeant didn't waste any time in raising his voice as his bulging blue eyes showed total exasperation. "I want some answers! The mayor doesn't like the growing victim list with the perpetrator still out there!" We looked at each other, not really sure who would speak first.

Wyla was the brave one. She spoke up. "From my boys and what I saw in Milwaukee, then taking into account what we learned today. The victim in Milwaukee has been identified as Romeo Blanco. We all saw from a camera in the back room of his restaurant that he left with a woman the day he disappeared."

"Sarg, we all know the woman he left with is Amora Rathbone, daughter to Ethan Rathbone, the billion-dollar CEO from IndyMerck." Luther added to the discussion.

"Can we connect from what happened in Milwaukee to the young woman butchered last night?" Gable asked.

"One thing for sure, the nature of the savagery…the form of cannibalism shows it could be the same killer." I said, having great difficulty in holding back a complete breakdown of emotion. I was fond of Katie Fisher, something in my training that was not recommended.

Mitch Gable got up from his desk chair, began to pace the space in front of us. "Let me lay this out from the last three and a half months. The attacks of the pregnant women came from some fantasy legend who had a specific agenda for unborn babies."

He stopped pacing, pointing to each one of us. "Now you tell me. This assailant has turned his or her agenda to murders of men or women with a cannibal stamp on it!"

"Sarg, the case has become pivotal. You well know. When my wife's liver was eaten partially away, I believe the assailant slightly turned more savage for a very good reason. What Althea and I found out in Algiers, outside of New Orleans, this "tik-tik" type of aswang eats babies from a belly entry into the womb as well as goes for devouring certain inner organs." Luther said, laying all the bizarre, out-there nature of the true name of what this suspect turned into.

"Sarg, we have all had so many bits of evidence pointing to this ancient legend with each victim. By your face and projecting attitude, I can feel your unbelief." I said, knowing he might throw us out in a rage.

Gable lowered his head, looking to be in deep thought. I felt a change in his agitation to a more pliable state. He paced again, in a soft tone of voice, "I'm sure, all of you have a specific person of interest in mind. Do what you can to sew up the loose ends for a solid action to bring the suspect in with a firm case of its guilt to all the victims. Don't talk about what you have told me this evening with anyone!" He waved us on to disappear out of his office. I felt but didn't share that our sergeant had much pondering to do on what we had laid out to him.

The weekend was here. Wyla, Luther and I agreed to map out a strategy separately. We were to compare notes on Monday. I made up my mind no matter how far out from my years of training, I had to see this through until she was caught, made powerless, and brought in. Let the courts decide what to do with such a criminal—the public would be shocked at such a beautiful looking and professionally successful woman who came from the best of families could perform such heinous acts of violence and cannibalism. I knew it was going to be difficult to relax enough to fall asleep. When alone in the solace of my apartment, I would see the images of the condition of Katie Fisher. Her pale eyes faded by death still open. The lower part of her body torn to shreds.

This case had put a knife into my soul. I felt like a mentally tortured victim. Amora Rathbone had purposely changed her mode of behavior to get to me. That day in July she looked into my eyes as she was going to ascend to her cold Tower. She decided to torture and damage the one thing in my life I was proud of—my job. I wasn't going to let her succeed.

Chapter Seventeen

Late Night Work

When Ethan Rathbone was at his wit's end, work helped to calm the upheaval of his recent feeling of hopelessness. The phone on his desk beeped. Knowing his secretary had gone home hours ago, he clicked the red flashing button.

"Sir, this is Walter from the parking gate. Are you getting ready to leave anytime soon? It's going on midnight." The young man said.

"I understand, Walter. I've got my card to open the gate. You go ahead and get out of here. Thank you." Ethan politely instructed.

Ethan got up. He took a break by looking out onto the city lights from the sixteenth floor windows. Going over again what transpired at yesterday morning's confrontation with his daughter, he realized any hopes on the drug's success to address this ancient curse had come to an impasse.

In the last six weeks, he knew his daughter's nightly hunts had turned to a savage end of unconscionable manifestations of a ghoulish creature. Tears rolled down his cheeks. A thought came to mind before he finished up. He needed to write an email to his lawyer.

TO: Forrest Baines, atty. at law

If there arises an unfortunate demise to my person, alert my faithful butler and friend, Wesley Thornton. He has no knowledge of the change to my last Will & Testament to the Rathbone assets, holdings and current residence to go to him.

My Kindest Regards,

Ethan Rathbone, CEO of IndyMerck Pharmaceuticals

A weariness surrounded Ethan. It was time to go home. His brand new Lexus shined out like a beacon from the dark sky above in the center of the employee parking lot. He stepped out from the double doors to find out he was the only one around.

He heard a low-pitched ticking sound not too far away. His heart sank. Thinking to himself almost a prayer, *Oh, Lord, got to get to my car. Maybe I can out run it.*

Three yards from the driver's side of his car, the ticking became so loud—it was painfully deafening. In seconds, he was wrapped in the black netting of an impenetrable substance of what he knew to be wings of the creature he knew so well. He felt the vacuum of being high in the night sky.

During the night flight, Ethan was forced to breathe in and out the surrounding foul odor of the material that held him immovable. He could hardly breathe and could not move or cry out. He remembered the rare times he had climbed up the cold three levels of the stone staircase to the Tower quarters.

Inside the room only furnished by a soiled mattress, the smell of sweat, vomit and finally the stench of decomposition hit his nose. He fled the interior of where the creature found sanctuary until the effects of her transformation brought her to be a human again.

He was unable to move as the winged creature unloaded him onto damp ground. The wings unfolded and parted away where the terrorized middle-age man viewed his captor. The full moon above reflected its illumination to reveal half of the creature's grotesque facial features.

In the past, Ethan had been told from his wife Divinia a description of this type of aswang. No one could have ever been prepared to the terror griping deep into their soul as this evil was revealed for real—the eyes reptilian bulging with a line of blinding yellow instead of the human pupil.

Its head moved back and forth, taking in Ethan's fear. The mouth opened to a protruding red tongue curled out partly through, showing upper and lower set of teeth formed in razor-sharp fangs.

"Amora, if any inkling of humanity can hear me, don't destroy your father. I've fought for you since your adolescence to keep your affliction secret!" Ethan pleaded, choking on his many tears.

Holding him still with her long claws, her head plunged down to tear away the middle of his face. One claw raised to make a precise movement. She finished his life as one long sharp digit cut his throat almost to the point of decapitation.

The defining moment that she had killed her father in such a hideous manner was not recorded to be defined as wrong on her part. The savagery and ghoulish nature of this curse came to full circle where this man who had raised her and protected her came to be another victim.

Chapter Eighteen
Grandpa Pete

Lately, I have been begging off my Sunday brunches at Grandpa Pete's. I hesitated going straight to the front door. I walked over to the living room windows to see my grandfather seated at his white grand piano. He played the keys with a serene expression of sheer pleasure. In my upside down inner clock it had clouded my sharpness of wit. I didn't think my presence would be suitable for breaking bread with him.

I heard a woman's voice calling my name, "Glenda, you silly, stop peeping at your grandfather's living room windows. Come to the door, dear."

The voice cajoling me came from Pete's latest lady friend, Grace. A widow who lived three houses down from him. I jumped, feeling like she had caught me smoking as a high school teacher of mine did many years ago.

I stood at the open door. "In my mood today, I don't know if I would be good company."

"Nonsense, we've fixed your favorite, chicken dressing casserole." Grace said, grabbing my left arm.

Grandpa Pete must have heard Grace at the front door. He met us in the formal dining room. "Glenda, looks like you haven't slept in days!

You're too young to have dark bags under your eyes." He said, pulling out a chair for me.

I attempted to steer him off the subject of my present physical appearance. "What were you playing?"

"Oh, I was doing my own syncopation of *Alley Cat*."

"Well, it sounded really good."

"Both of you sit down. I'll bring in the hot casserole. You can dig into the salads. Don't be shy, Glenda." Grace interrupted our small talk.

I waited until she had disappeared into the kitchen. "She looks like she has taken over."

"Funny, I'm getting to like it. At this point in my life, a woman puttering around this big house is comforting to me. Don't scoff at her. She's genuinely fond of you." He said, his face full of contentment.

I did not realize how hungry I had been for a home cooked meal and frivolous conversation. I was starting to feel somewhat normal. These days that was a rarity. Grandpa Pete got up then bent over and kissed Grace. This was something I hadn't been a witness to, ever. I was beginning to feel a warmth towards Grace.

He raised up and asked me, "Do you want some espresso to top off the meal?"

"Yes, that would be great."

I wanted to thank Grace for such a tasty and enjoyable brunch when she spoke up. "Are you getting any closer to catching this vile attacker?"

I replied in a dry type of answer. "Well, there is a task force working on all angles of the case. We have many theories, nothing iron-clad yet."

"You need to step up, my dear. I've been friends with Melanie Rossen for years. She hasn't been herself since that attack in June. Now, I hear about, these attacks have turned to savage murders!" She rambled on, showing some agitation with her voice getting to a shrill.

Grandpa Pete came back with two small mugs of espresso. "Here you go, detective. What have you ladies been chatting about?"

Grace answered in a condescending tone. "Glenda's been giving me unsatisfactory knowledge on her present long-suffering investigation. I'm sure with more victims losing their lives."

"Grace, you've got to realize a detective has the right to hold back on details to avoid a city panic." My grandfather said, attempting to come to my rescue.

Grace sat there silent, glaring at me. She drank the remainder of her ice water with those disapproving grayish-blue eyes. I could not sit there any longer. I left my espresso half full. That warmth for Grace a few minutes ago turned quickly into disdain. I stood up. "Thank you both for an enjoyable brunch."

Grandpa Pete followed me to the front door. He grabbed me before I went out the door, probably slamming it in my present state. "Honey, you need to give Grace some levity. There are those who possess great fear since glimpses of this case have spread in the last few months."

I said to myself, *What's the use. I could stand here and give my grandfather a viable argument. I was too angry and too frustrated.* I raised up and gave him a kiss on his forehead. "Pete, I'm happy you found somebody, really."

I got in my car, sat there a bit before starting it up. Grace did bring forth a factor I could act on. Melanie Rossen was not getting any better mentally. Her emotional and mental scares were far from being healed as her physical body had done. I found myself in and around Anderson University campus on the east side of the city. I stood at her front door, ringing her doorbell nervous. Knowing I would not be well received, I had to take whatever Melanie would put out towards me.

Manfred Foy opened the door. "Why detective, it's been awhile. What can I do for you?"

"I apologize for the sudden visit. Can I talk to Melanie?"

"Yes, follow me. She's reading back in the rose garden." He graciously let me in.

We walked through the double sliding glass doors from the kitchen. Melanie's back was to me as I walked out onto the stone terrace getting a full view of the several varieties of rose bushes arranged in half-moon rows in the square back yard.

She had heard the opening of the doors, peeking her head around her lawn chair. With a sour expression discovering I was behind Professor Foy. She said. "Well, Manny, it seems you brought some kind of pitiful looking law enforcement officer to my sanctuary."

I was right. She was not happy to see me. Mustered all my courage, I pulled up a chair to her direct left. "Thank you for not screaming me away. I needed to see you."

She slapped her book down on the white wrought-iron table to her right. "Well, the last time I saw you. Amado and you were obviously into some kind of upcoming tryst with no word from you about how much you enjoyed our gracious dinner invitation. I guess, your investigation takes precedence over looking in on that thing's live victims."

Manfred gave us privacy sneaking slowly away into the house. I ignored her sour attitude towards me, and continued on. "I've been very lapse on checking back with you. You are absolutely right. How have you been since that dinner at Vera Mae's?"

"Well, I've been knee deep into research about what attacked me. Funny, even the worst of what I've learned keeps me from going over the deep end. Sometimes my night terrors are excruciating. Manny helps since we have gotten married." She said.

"Congratulations on your marriage. That's got to be one good result from this nightmare." I told her, hoping to break her icy stare.

"Detective, what have you really come for?" Melanie asked.

"I'm with you on the night terrors. The deeper I go with this case. I experience nightly images invading my sleep causing me to soak my sheets with sweat. Not able to go back to sleep, I take up my sketch book and drew out the images. One of the last victims not only was attacked but savagely murdered. The identity of the him showed up in my sketch book."

I stopped, then I did something I rarely do. I cried in front of someone. Melanie turned to face me, then put her hand on my arm. I said to her. "I'm not supposed to tell you this but the last victim, Katie Fisher had been torn to pieces in her bathroom. I almost lost my shit in front of navy blue officers at the scene."

"My Sweet Christ, that sweet waitress from The Bobber's Café?" Melanie gasped in shock.

"I was so fond of her. Somehow my strong attraction to Amado makes me feel responsible for her death."

"No, I found out much later after that dinner, Amado is something of a supernatural mystery. I have done a great deal of study especially when it comes to the ability of the creature to shapeshift. The magic arts are strong enough for the cursed woman to change into a man. She can change into a form of a man when it suits her as well as manifesting into the aswang." Melanie said something so bizarre, I stopped feeling sorry for myself enough to get the full import of what she had learned in the last weeks.

"Let me get what you are saying. What hunted you out was really a woman who had shifted into the figure of a man." I said, leaning back into my chair. My face held a stare almost like I was in a trance.

"Glenda, in the form of the creature, the aswang, there was this muscled torso. That is why I told you it was a man that attacked me. When in actuality, the shapeshifting phenomenon had the ability to fool me to think a man attacked me for his specific propose. The aswang is really a woman."

I began to sweat. My mouth became so dry it was hard to swallow. I wanted to speak but found it difficult. Melanie read on my face I was in a grave panic. She got up from her lawn chair and went to the glass sliding doors. "Manny, come quickly."

He came to her side immediately. "Manny, I'm going to get the detective a goblet of sherry. Sit with her. She's in a state."

Manny pulled up another lightweight lawn chair. He asked me very softly. "What can I do for you, detective?" I was too overcome with the news about Amado/Amora mind-fuck to reply.

Melanie got to me, and handed me the sherry. "Take small sips."

In a few minutes, I was able to speak. "What you told me was quite the shocker. I shouldn't be surprised at anything related to this blasted legend. So, the man Amado who kissed my lips and later came to my apartment one night was really Amora." I took two more sips. "Jesus on the cross! She could have killed me right then and there."

Manny spoke up. "You know, detective. There is a strange reason why she spared your life. Maybe after so long she wants to be free from this curse, whether to be destroyed or somehow a way to rid herself of being this horrible "Mr. Hyde" creature. She knows you will not stop until this thing is in prison."

The sherry was soothing not only to the inside of my mouth but I was able to slowly calm down. I could begin to think clear, to think analytically like I always did in my work. Ironic, at the beginning of this investigation, the woman who sat here helping me to regain some kind of sanity was the woman I wanted to discredit.

I took her hands, and tears came forth again. "Both of you have been so kind, even though I've been such a shit!"

Melanie spoke. "Glenda, before I acquired this knowledge about my assailant, I was toying with the idea of suicide. We have to fight against this evil in our separate fashion. I do it with getting ahold of the most information I can, and giving myself time to enjoy a new life with Manny. You do it by putting aside any previous wrong thought processes and find a way to bring her in. Not so much to destroy her in the same bloody fashion she has done to all her victims. Bring her before the justice system no matter how hard it will be."

I went back to my apartment, watching the sun set from my living room long overstuffed couch. The lavender and deep orange mix gave way to a darker indigo. I realized the fantasies I harbored for the type of man I thought Amado was, became more attractive than his actual physicality. I decided then and there to embrace what I had to do. There was my reputation as a capable detective on the line. My mind faced the reality to grip hard on the dynamics of what would entail a pursuit of a supernatural creature who possessed not only nibble abilities of rapid movement but a backlog of magical powers I was ignorant of.

Until I could let sleep overtake me, I read a brief Luther had written in the last two weeks. He detailed various ways this creature in full manifestation could be brought to a brief time of stagnation in order to experience a brutal ritual of ridding the cursed phenomenon of what contaminated its inner core. I got through three-fourths of a detailed account with full knowledge, I would be terrified in every aspect of this unusual pursuit and seizure.

Chapter Nineteen

A Group Is Formed

Somewhat refreshed from a rare night of sleep, I walked into my division prepared for some strategy. I was convinced to act quickly, no matter how far afield my burning desire to see this through. I entered the break room where Luther and Wyla were drinking coffee.

I began talking without permission. "Wyla, you're theory about Amado Rathbone is mute. I found out some revealing and bizarre details yesterday."

George came bursting in, holding a short stack of glossy 3"x5" photographs. He brought them up to my face. "I got these developed from the autopsy in Milwaukee. Detective, look at this particular one."

What I viewed gave me quite a shock but at the same time revealed much. The photograph was a close up of the victim's face, or what was left. His right eye, nose, and mouth were no longer there, looking like a jagged missing puzzle piece.

Fighting back complete revulsion, I kept staring and recognized the left eye. Here from this shocking image, we had solid confirmation of the identity of the victim. I shouted, "It's official. That is Romeo Blanco. I could not forget those dreamy deep rich color of his eyes when Luther and I first met him."

All the photos including the one I made such a fuss about were passed around to Wyla and Luther. Wyla said, "I think, Glenda you are perfectly correct. We have a green light to go after Ms. Rathbone."

George spoke up, "I think us guys are in. You three have been tiptoeing around us about who this Rathbone chick really is. We need full disclosure to join the ranks."

Wyla, Luther and I looked at each other. Wyla looked at George, and nodded, "Round up the guys. To call her out means there are specific guidelines to be discussed in detail." She turned to Luther and I. "George, the three of us held our belief to ourselves for a reason. What we will disclose to you guys is so bizarre, it is going to take a lot for you to believe us."

One of the interrogation rooms was empty. I put a "Do Not Disturb" sign on the glass window while Luther disengaged the overhead camera and intercom devices. First, as the guys brought in extra chairs around the small square table, Wyla brought out several bits of evidence with the victim list that verified the "Special Person Of Interest" to be this human cursed to become the supernatural creature with an ancient past.

All three sat there apparently in deep thought as Luther began talking. "If we choose to bring her in, we have to implement a finely orchestrated course of action."

The agent John asked. "From what I believe of you embracing this woman turning into this monster, how do we proceed?"

"I need to know, since you guys are going to join us crazed fighters of such evil. What the hell are your real names?" I interrupted.

John said. "My real name is Bertram Little."

Paul said. "My real name is Irving Nussbaum."

George said with a smirk. "My name is Octavian Lancer."

I looked at Luther and Wyla. "Wow! I can see why Wyla penned those Beatle names to you. I guess we will leave it at that, John, Paul, and George."

Wyla pointed to me, saying, "Glenda and Luther have a way of contacting Amora Rathbone. We are going to call her out. If she takes the bait, we will go about apprehending her at the park where all the attacks began."

"A shaman or Filipina holy woman who talked to Althea and I in Algiers sent me four jars of a solution to leave her powerless for a short time." Luther disclosed.

George asked, "How much time do we have to bring her in? Will she still be like vamped out?"

I responded. "It is important that she be in her beastly form. Before we bring her in, we have to string her up with heavy cable onto a strong thick branch. Beat her back between her wings until this form of a chick spews out of her mouth."

John shouted with an alarmed expression, "For Christ Sake, that sounds barbaric!"

Wyla jumped out of her seat. "We are dealing with an evil our agented experience has not come across ever! All of us have to realize banning together, we need to put what we've been trained out to pasture. This suspect is defined to be something that could possibly take all of us over with the horror, right in your face!"

All of us became silent for some minutes. Wyla's words were not only sobering but made us question our inner courage when faced with something so grotesque and so savage. Paul got up, then went to stand in front of the chart I had propped up on an easel.

"I can climb a tree. If the creature gets cornered, I can pour that jar stuff onto its back. Of course, getting as close as I can to where the wings intersect. A difficult bloody bullseye, I must insist."

"Since this fiend has it out for me, I will expose myself enough for her to chase me to the spot we pick to surround her. A month ago, a giant tree split in two from a passing tornado. We can locate that tree, and map out how we can get her to that precise spot. Knowing the park system in this city, the broken branches haven't been hauled away yet." I said.

All of us were about to head out to Shadyside Park. Mitch Gable ignored the sign and opened the door. He directed his reason for interrupting us with an alarming statement.

"Glenda and Luther, I got off the phone with Indy Metro chief. He wants you two to meet a couple of his detectives at Marion County Coroner Office." Mitch said.

"Can we go along?" Wyla asked.

"No can do. This gentleman, Wesley Thornton emphasized on Glenda and Luther only."

No argument, and I did not venture any questions towards Mitch. His expression and body language read to me, he was not in the mood for any type of discussion. We drove to the county coroner's office building, a brand new facility on West McCarty Street, downtown Indianapolis. As we entered the lobby, two Indy Metro detectives approached us.

Both had the odd look in their plain clothes-suit and tie attire that they would be more comfortable wearing striped overalls with a white dirty T-shirt underneath. The older one with a balloon-belly and a striped red tie poorly put together spoke up. "My partner and I will escort you to the Observation Area, a bit of a maze of corridors. So bear with us."

The lightness of the painted walls over a noticeable concrete block possessed newness. Graphic signs of where we were to be headed appeared with each left or right direction going into an ongoing corridor until we finally came to an arrow above which read, "Observation Room". One of the detectives offered us a short explanation as we went through the stainless steel heavy door. "This discrete area has been created for families to identify the recent brought in body, and also a way police and prosecutors can view and study the body before and during an autopsy."

We saw Wesley Thornton and a tall morgue technician dressed in a long lightweight white coat standing over a sheeted body on top of a long rectangular stainless steel table. No matter how new this facility appeared to me, and the overall clinical feeling surrounding us. It was still a morgue. The coldness of the room hit my nostrils as if I had put my head into the freezer section of a local grocery store.

I looked at Wesley, we shared a quiet exchange with a polite nod. His body language was his usual stiff and professional stance as his station in the Rathbone household. His eyes were red from lack of sleep and apparent bouts of tearing up.

The man in the long white coat spoke as the Metro detectives, Luther and I took our respective positions around the sheeted corpse. "I take it the Metro detective have brought in Detective McMahan and Detective Charles in from the APD in Anderson. Mr. Thornton didn't want to begin until you arrived."

The sheet was removed. No one uttered a sound, but it was as if some unforeseen entity gasped surrounding all of us with a cloud of shock and dismay at what we were about to discover. Wesley Thornton nodded, speaking in a tone of somberness on the verge of breaking down into heavy sobs. "Yes, this is Ethan Rathbone."

Luther gagged, taking an exit from close to the victim to an area across the room near a work area. I stood there studying the dead man's face. The remains of how it appeared reminded me of Romeo Blanco's face or the lack of it. Ethan Rathbone's face was only there with his left eye, left cheek, and chin remaining. This shocking picture confirmed this to be "Victim Number Twenty-Eight".

The younger ginger-haired Metro detective asked Wesley. "Do you want to have some privacy before we take you to headquarters?"

"No, sir, I'm ready to comply. I would like Detective McMahan and Detective Charles to be there for the interrogation."

Luther and I followed the detective's vehicle with Wesley Thornton in the backseat to Metro headquarters on North Alabama Street. We quietly followed the detectives and Wesley through some hallways into a small interrogation room equipped with appropriate tables and chairs, and to our surprise an overstuffed red arm chair and matching sofa.

The young ginger-haired detective introduced himself as Detective Matthew Felts. The older bulky detective followed by introducing himself as Detective Vernon Lutz. Wesley sat in the red upholstered chair in front of the detectives seated at the ends of the square table. Luther and I took our seats at the sofa to the side of Wesley.

Detective Lutz began the interrogation of Wesley. "What is your relationship to the victim, Ethan Rathbone?"

"I have been Master Rathbone's butler for the last thirty-five years. In that time we have become very close."

"The coroner gave us a timeline of how long Mr. Rathbone was dead before his discovery on the Monon Trail, four days from September 28th. Where were you at this time?" Detective Felts asked.

"I spent the evening with Clarissa Ross, Amora Rathbone's secretary at Saxony Research Facility."

"Can we get her to corroborate your statement?"

"Yes, detective, by all means, she will tell you I was with her all night."

I agreed to hold back, but I could not help myself. "Detectives, I have one question that could connect a victim found in Milwaukee. Can I proceed with Mr. Thornton?"

The detectives looked at each other and nodded. I faced Wesley and asked. "Mr. Thornton, do you have a revealing knowledge of the murder of Romeo Blanco?"

"Yes, I do. I was there when he was murdered. I drove the couple sitting in the back seat to a dense woods outside of Milwaukee." Wesley calmly said, staring intently at the noticeably shocked pair of Metro detectives.

Detective Felts stopped himself from falling onto the hard tile floor. He said, "Mr. Thornton, you will have to remain in our custody until we get a chance to discuss what you've told us to the authorities at Milwaukee District 1."

Detective Lutz stayed in the room with Wesley Thornton while Detective Felts escorted Luther and I outside into the hallway. "Detectives, could you send us an overview of your case so far?"

"I can fax over a brief I compiled when we get back to our division." Luther said.

"Whoa! Detective Felts, just one minute! Are we going to continue to be a party to anymore of your questioning of Mr. Thornton?" I probed rather strongly.

"Our hands are tied. We will not be asking any more questions until we hear from Milwaukee. From what he confessed, he will most likely be extradited up north. Both of you full well know this to be true." He said, insisting in his expression with a downward positioning of his bushy eyebrows.

Detective Lutz spoke to Wesley. "You are not arrested just held for further questions. I need to advise you call a lawyer if you already have one in mind."

I realized I better back down. Luther silently agreed with them, by putting a vice-grip on my right elbow. I took his cue and, we drove back to Anderson. Most of the drive north, I was silently steaming inside.

"I realize Glenda, what you're thinking." Luther said as he entered I69 North.

"Once those detectives read your outrageous and not-to-be-believed brief, they will pin those murders of Blanco and Ethan Rathbone on Wesley." I ranted on.

"So, this is what we will do. All of us, FBI agents, you and I will go as planned. I advise you to calm down and really concentrate. If we are successful in bringing Amora in, it will take the heat off of Wesley. Besides, he is safer in police custody." Luther carefully sorted it out, making perfect sense.

I took a large glass and poured an ice cold Rolling Rock into it. I mulled over in my mind each step the group of us would take tomorrow night. I don't know if it was the beer or the protocol each one of us would accomplish to pull off what to most law enforcement officers defined to be "bat-shit crazy". I put the half drank glass on the coffee table and curled up on my couch. In minutes, I was asleep.

Chapter Twenty-One

Rendezvous with Evil

In order for me not to turn back on this unusually warm October night, I had to go over every detail of the group plan in my head. Otherwise I would be wrapped up in my silk orchid quilted comforter shaking in sheer panic and shame of not joining my compatriots.

Luther, Wyla, George, John and Paul were all issued tranquilizer guns—non-lethal air gun equipped with a .50 caliber ballistic syringe. Each gun's hypodermic syringe was filled with the solution of ground mandrake root and bull semen to incapacitate Amora when fully transformed. I, on the other hand was not holding a small plastic tube of the tranquilizing solution in my right pocket. I was the pawn to take on decoy position as "lone victim".

I parked my car at the entrance off of Cross St., where most of the fishing boats launch from. I got out of the car. Looking up at the full moon, I took in the subtle beauty resembling a giant blue and white marble in the sky. I stared into a wall of thick-leaved trees. Paralyzing fear gripped me as I could see complete darkness in between the clusters of yellow, green, and orange leaves.

I shook my head, telling myself to stay with the program. I called Luther. "I'm here at the Cross St. entrance. I am beginning on foot now."

I put my iPhone in my back pocket, swallowed, felt a lump in my throat and sudden craving for a diet Dr. Pepper.

The winding trail became more dense and narrow as I knew from past experience. On my left was a slight incline down to the embankment of the lake, and to my right was the winding White River. I noticed something odd—the twelve-foot black painted lamplighter street lamps put every sixty feet were not illuminated. A streak of panic ran through me.

I noticed there were no noises of crickets in the grass on each side of me. There wasn't any birds flying overhead. This state of complete silence was odd and made me think, she was near.

Every other step I opened my phone to illuminate going forward. Coming to a small blue-painted steel bridge, I heard ticking overhead. My mouth became dry, and my heart beat fast and hard. I looked above only seeing parts of the dark navy purple sky from the dense groupings of tree branches overlapping.

The ticking became almost deafening. In the next few moments, I felt extreme sharpness onto both of my shoulders. I was being lifted into the sky in seconds—reflections of the full moon gave me a view of these large black bone-structure of what was revealed to be giant bat wings.

I don't know what made me to do this, maybe fear and instinct of some kind. I screamed up to my captor. "I knew you would come for me. If there is any humanity left in you, I saw what you did to your father!"

Luther and Wyla were leaning up against Althea's smaller car, Kia Soul. They heard a sound at first could be identified as a small plane. In a few minutes they heard a screeching sound with a combination of ticking so loud they thought their eardrums would burst. To their horror, they saw a winged creature fly over them at the red covered bridge site. Wyla pulled up her binoculars to view this creature had me held in its large sharp talons.

Luther called John who was high in one of the sycamore trees that was to be defined as the place of contact. "The creature has Glenda, and is on its way to you and Paul."

Blood began flowing with constant drips into my eyes, I assumed from my shoulders. We reached the area where the giant sycamore tree had been broken in several places. Strange, the creature landed to the ground in front of the network of broken branches. It was as if she read my mind that this was the precise location I wanted her to be. I found myself on the warm ground held down by the creature's clawed hands. The clawed hands smelled musty like a damp basement covered in cobwebs and dirt.

I glanced up to see John high in one of the neighboring trees to the left of the central place of the broken tree where a jagged edge of a thick branch was sticking up higher than the others. I was hoping Paul was on the other side. My vision was impaired as the creature got close to my face.

An eerie voice came out of the mouth full of sharp fangs. Not only did I have to take in the frightening sight of a grotesque creature who towered over me, but the voice audible brought my fear to a whole new level of terror.

From an unnerving combination of ticking and the sound of a slow rattle much like a rattlesnake before it strikes, the creature spoke. "I decided to become Amado to pursue you time and time again. I could feel your vulnerability for a beautiful man. I wanted you to torture yourself inside because you wanted to love him but you knew you would not dare. I'm going to tear your flesh slowly now because you angered me. You interrupted my feeding season."

With that said, the red tongue coiled out, touching my nose, cheeks, and lips. The odor from the thick liquid off of the tongue surface possessed a horrid stench. I had smelled it before when Wyla and I secretly entered the room in the Rathbone Tower where there was only a soiled mattress. I braced myself for thinking the creature was getting ready to begin the tearing with my face.

The head and face raised up, then with one swoop of movement the left clawed hand sliced my left side from my rib cage down to my knee. The movement was swift. My brain did not register any pain yet. My eyes were too busy watching John and Paul simultaneously pulled down their guns and shooting the creature in the center of where the wings intersected.

I saw the creature's reptilian yellowish-red eyes looking stunned. Its head turned around as another shot hit the creature in the throat. That shot came from George facing the creature. The creature tried to get upright, stumbling backwards into the very part of the broken branch that was calculated to help in incapacitating it temporarily. I laid there in shock and awe. Broken curved branches of all shapes and sizes moved slightly to form a natural cage to keep the creature held. I got a comforting thought, nature was fighting against the evil it held captive.

George bent down and asked me. "Glenda, can you move at all?"

"Yes, I think, but I'm a bloody mess. Help me up."

John and Paul climbed down. George and I moved towards the immovable creature held captive by the gnarled network of broken branches.

John turned around to announce. "Here's Luther and Wyla. Their timing is perfect."

George went rattling on as he took several photos from his iPhone. "Let me get as many as I can before we string it up. Not sure, images of this thing hanging from a tree branch getting beaten with a bat will not over well with the FBI or the APD."

Luther got out of Althea's car, holding heavy black cable and traditional rough-surface rope. Wyla came out of the passenger side with a blanket and an aluminum bat.

John, Paul, and George bound up the creature's wings, arms, and legs with the rope. John climbed back up one of the larger trees, while Luther, George and Paul maneuvered the bulky grayish-green body to connect its bound up legs to the heavy cable.

I maneuvered my broken body over to a natural-formed bench from four broken branches. I was beginning to feel stabbing pains around my rib cage and down my left side. I held it together and concentrated on what was to happen next. I was very close to where the creature's head hung down from the overhead jutted out tree branch. I had a ringside seat to the "defrocking of a monster".

Wyla passed me with a trance-like stare. She held the bat as if it was a precious possession. "Let me do the honors. After all, this is payback for my ancestors being killed by these savage things."

Wyla used all her rage and strength to swing once, striking the upside-down creature in between where the wings intersected, high in its back. The second blow caused the creature to let out a strange squealing sound much like a wounded beast. With the third blow stronger than the last, I could see much pain in the face of the creature. More pathetic cries ensued, filling up our wooded surroundings with such sounds I was sure nearby residents could hear.

The creature's mouth opened, gagging commenced. I thought the cries were intolerable, its retching was worse. I was getting ready to command Wyla to stop. Then it happened—an object with a fluttering movement spewed out onto the paved trail.

All of us formed a circle. Luther helped me up to get a better view. The object looked like a newly hatched duck totally black, and hairless. Close study the structure of the hairless duckling, there were indications of webbing in between its feet—like a tiny dragon. It's mouth opened, as if it needed air or food. I felt sick looking at this delicate grotesque thing. Before anyone knew what to say or do next, Wyla set the small thing on fire with her pocket lighter.

Shouting at Wyla, hurt with every breath. "Why did you do that? We need that little creature as evidence!"

Wyla shrugged her shoulders and said. "I was in the moment. Sorry, Glen. We can gather the ashes and bones left."

George yelled. "Oh, guys. Look what is happening to the creature!"

We moved swiftly from the burned up the duckling, George quickly doused the flames. We watched the creature turn from the monster we had captured to the face of Amado Rathbone, then to the face of Amora Rathbone. Was she fully human? Time would give us the answer.

George cut her down while John and Paul lowered her slowly to the trail as Luther covered her naked body with a blanket. Wyla was putting the ashes and bones of the duckling into a plastic bag. Then Wyla came up to me with another plastic bag and a pocket knife. "Glenda, hold still.

I'm going to get some torn flesh from your shoulder for testing. We need all the evidence we can get. There are going to be some skeptics coming out of the woodwork to crucify all of us."

I cannot deny the small amount of skin she took from my exposed skin, hurt like nothing I had ever experienced before. Still it was for the case. Afterwards, I reeled some to the point of landing on the ground once again. Wyla showed no concern, her face mesmerized by gathering the evidence of her brutality to the creature.

George and Luther saw my body weaving. They were getting worried at my deteriorating appearance. They grilled me about if I would be better off being taken to the hospital only three miles up from where we were. I insisted with intensity of stubbornness. "I'm not going to miss the fun of her being taken in. I will meet you guys there. Leave me be!"

I drove to the Detective Division struck with a sinking feeling in the pit of my stomach. I should have been relieved that we achieved our goal. I talked out loud to myself, "Well, I'm not dead. She didn't get her way tearing me limb from limb. Why do I feel like my world is about to cave in?"

Amora Rathbone was escorted to the front desk of the division by Luther and Wyla. The navy suit officer stood there in total alarm of this petite closed-mouthed dark haired brown-skinned woman wrapped in a burgundy blanket held in handcuffs. He stood there with his mouth opened.

"Officer Faraday, this is Amora Rathbone who has been apprehended this evening from Shadyside Park. She happens to be the suspect of the many attacks and murders plaguing Anderson, Indianapolis, and Milwaukee. We are taking her to the closest interrogation room. Which one is available, my good man?" Luther asked.

"Oh, right, Detective Charles. Room 8 is available." Officer Faraday answered.

Wyla spoke up, "Officer, she will need some clothes, probably a size 6 in women's. Let Mitch Gable know where we are."

I came in right after Faraday had called the sergeant. Breathless, I came up to the front desk. He spoke before I did. "Glenda, they took the suspect to Room 8. Don't you think you need an ambulance. You're all torn up!"

I waved him off. "Oh, I'll be good." I smiled at him.

My wounds from the creature began to bring forth excruciating pain. I felt very weak. I snapped my fingers at Faraday. "I'm beginning to agree with you about having to go to the hospital. Get a message to my partner Luther. Tell him to get ahold of Unc Monroe."

After I got that out, I had crumbled down to the floor like a rag doll.

Chapter Twenty-Two
The Upside Down Of It All

Frightening images flashed, tugging at my perception of what is real, and what isn't. Flights of terror so unnerving, they defied my highest threshold of imagination. I saw giant skeletal flying apparatus on either side of my peripheral vision to resemble what I had learned in middle school Biology class as wings belonging to a bat. I was held in a state between unconsciousness and a slight realization of my reality I had always known.

In my dreamlike mind, I actually felt the hardness of asphalt on my back and head. The creature I remembered to have made myself a decoy to opened its mouth. It showed such methodical precision signaling my time on earth was coming to an end. I felt like sobbing, weeping profusely—this end to be riddled with the very same agony all those other victims experienced where their flesh was being slowly ripped apart.

I thrashed around, screaming inside. I found out soon, I was screaming out loud. In between screams, I heard a familiar voice saying my name several times.

"Glenda, Glenda, Glenda, please stop. It's Grandpa Pete with Unc. You're safe now. We are with you in a hospital room at St. Vincent's."

I opened my eyes, trying to lift my body up from my present safe asylum of fresh hospital pillows and linen. Two strong square hands gently placed me back down onto the fluffy mound of pillows. I began to know, it was Grandpa Pete. I blinked then saw Unc Monroe smiling down on me next to my grandfather.

"Unc, you got my message. I promised you I would let you know after all that happened." I said, struggling a smile.

"You and your officer party, sure did the job, my beauty." Unc told me with tears in his eyes.

"What am I doing here? Last time I knew, I was talking to fat Faraday."

"My girl, Faraday was the one who called the ambulance from the detective division. You were all torn up and fainted like a stone onto the floor in front of his desk." Grandpa Pete said.

I threw off the top sheet and blanket. I suddenly felt a jolt of pain in my shoulders, then turned to my left and noticed the feeling of constant pain all along my left side. "Oh, Lord Sakes, do I ever hurt!"

"You were in surgery for three hours. They had to suture your jagged skin from so many gashes on your shoulders and your left side. I was told from Luther, you volunteered to be the decoy." Pete said, fighting back tears.

I was starting to feel my brain remember what happened. "Yeah, she was out to tear me apart for what she said, I interrupted her feeding season. I do remember now. George shot the third application into her neck."

"Glenda, you keeping saying her. Are you referring to the woman under custody? She is one strange character, won't talk only to shout someone kept beating her."

"Pete, she is Amora Rathbone in full manifestation of that vile creature who attacked all those women, and then savagely killed Romeo Blanco, Katie Fisher, and then her own father Ethan Rathbone! It was what you heard about when you were stationed in the Philippines."

Grandpa Pete sat down at my side. Unc slide a chair over and sat on my other side. He patted my hand several times to calm me down. Grandpa Pete said. "Listen to me! Mitch called me yesterday while you were in and out of consciousness after surgery. I've decided to come out of retirement to represent you and Luther."

I pointed to the water pitcher sitting on the bed tray. I guzzled down half of the filled glass. I still had tremendous pain. "I've got to have something for the pain so I can process what you have told me!"

Grandpa Pete picked up the remote hanging from the right side of the bed. He hit the button for the nurse. Didn't take long, the nurse assigned to my room showed up at my door. I struggled to lift up. She came to my side. "Let's get you comfortable. Now, what's going on?"

"I'm hurting like a son-of-a-bitch!" I said, then cowered when I realized I shouted an obscenity in the presence of Grandpa Pete and Unc.

The nurse looked at my grandfather and Unc. "I will be right back with some pain medicine. It's been over ten hours."

I stared at my grandfather. "Wyla took it upon herself to beat the back of the creature several times with a bat. We had all been told by some holy woman that this would force the chick out of the cursed one to break it."

"Meaning to break the curse. Did that happen?"

"It sure did. This strange looking duckling with inklings of dragon like wings and feet came out. Wyla burned it up with her lighter." I said in a calmer frame of mind.

"This is sure a fantastical account. Mitch had told me she changed into the clothes brought to her in the interrogation room. There were bruises across her back discovered by Luther and Wyla. That fact stopped any questioning. The only words she uttered were ones of wanting to see her father." Grandpa Pete told me.

At that moment, the nurse brought in a small white cup of two Percasetts. I swallowed down fast. "Thank you so much, nurse. I apologize for yelling at you."

She nodded and smiled back. "I will leave you to your visitors. Don't be long, you need as much rest as possible."

Waiting until the nurse disappeared. I got back to Grandpa Pete. "I take it, Luther and I will have brutality charges leveled at us, as well as the FBI agents." He said nothing, only nodded.

Wyla popped her head into the door opening, "Can I join in?"

Grandpa Pete kissed me on the forehead. Unc got up and followed my grandfather out the door. "I'll let you ladies talk. I'll be back tomorrow, my girl." Grandpa Pete waved as he and Unc disappeared out into the hospital corridor.

Wyla waltzed in, carrying a plant arrangement. She placed it on the movable bed tray. "I figured you could use this at your apartment when you mend all the way."

I nodded, then didn't waste any time by opening up to our recent dilemma. "Pete told me about the pending charges leveled at us. Where are you going from here?"

She shrugged her shoulders and walked over to the double windows a few paces from my bed. "John, George, Paul and myself have been given our orders to report back to the Chicago office. We will go through some half-baked hearing. If we all land with our badges taken away, I'm considering joining the boys in Paris."

"What's in Paris?" I asked, not expecting that kind of an answer.

She turned around to face me. She came over to the right side of my bed. "George has this contact in the city, of savage murders taking place from the Paris Underground." She leaned in with a look of excitement. "Details point to another tik-tik, this one has a yen for human flesh."

"I would think you would rest some and go to an exotic island somewhere in the Caribbean."

"My young detective, I'm not the garden variety of an agent. I don't take off on exotic vacations after a difficult case. But what you need to get your head around our recent truth. None of us will ever do the normal again. What we have seen and especially the bizarre thing we saw the other night at the park will not ever leave us." Wyla tapped me on my hand.

"Besides, you might have some glimmer of hope you and Luther could get a jump on this closed-mouthed suspect. He has got a report from forensics. Ava Mead did tests on three samples of DNA, two I provided and the one this ER sent to them." She winked at me.

Wyla got up and made her way to the open door. I shouted at her/ "Now wait! Can't you tell me the results? I'll go crazy laying here wondering."

"Trust me, Luther wants to be the bearer of good tidings." She waved, giving over to a low-pitched girlish chuckle.

What a bomb to leave me with. I laid there, my eyes getting weary. Then the nurse came bouncing into the room. She checked my vitals. "Looks good. The doctor will be in any minute to check underneath the bandages."

As she made her way for her exit, a tall slightly balding man in a white doctor's long jacket came close to my left side. His large round eyes deep brown were warm and made me feel comforted with his easy bedside manner. He spoke with a slight accent.

"Detective, I'm Dr. Jetty. I was the surgeon who stitched up your shoulders and most of your left side. It took quite a long time. You were very torn up, but we got you through it. Let me take a look this afternoon."

He gently lifted off the gaze-like bandages. I felt a twinge of prickliness, no stabbing pains. He talked softly as his gloved hands examined my exposed areas affected by my savage attack. "When I first came to you in the ER, you fought hard against me doing anything until I extracted some blood-riddled loose skin for DNA. I've got to say, I was impressed by your reserve for pain. I obeyed your bidding."

"Did I sound hysterical or somewhat reasonable?"

"Your reasoning mind was sharp enough for me to take you seriously. I took the sample before we put you under. You detectives are so married to your jobs almost as much as us doctors." He said, showing amusement under his breath.

He turned to the nurse who walked back into the room, carrying a small tray. "Ms. Fadeley, she's all yours."

"Detective McMahan, before I leave. I can say, you are healing very well. I urge you not to return to work after being discharged. You're still not out of the woods where infections are concerned." He said, nodding then swiftly left the room.

Strange how the details of knowing the DNA was taken as I instructed, then Wyla confirming it. I did feel some relief, I did not meet the same end as Katie Fisher or Ethan Rathbone. I laid there as the nurse cleaned my many wounds and placed fresh bandages harboring impending doom to the outcome of my job and any detriment to my reputation.

I thought to myself. *Is this how a soldier feels when going through a bloody battle? I can validate the definition of going through a type of a war, a war of the ancients that still is true today. A war of good against evil with my war wounds to prove it.* The sweet expression of the young brunette nurse looked into my eyes, to reassure me. I would be alive another day.

Chapter Twenty-Three

Two Ways To Fight

A stocky distinguished white-haired man dressed in a shiny gray suit came walking into the Milwaukee District 1 headquarters, being directed to one of the dozen interrogations rooms down the hall from Detective Mason Doyle's office. Forrest Baines knocked on the closed door of Room 10, Detective Doyle's younger partner let him in. Wesley Thornton seated adjacent to Detective Doyle breathed a sigh of relief when he recognized Ethan Rathbone's lawyer.

"Mr. Baines, we did as you instructed on the phone. No questions until you arrived." Detective Doyle said.

Forrest Baines took a seat across the table from his client. "I need to know from you Detective Doyle the reason why my client was extradited here in Milwaukee."

"Sir, a week ago, Wesley Thornton had confessed to Indianapolis detectives he was there when Romeo Blanco was murdered. He complied to being under our custody." The detective said in a dry delivery.

"Well, detectives, I leave it to you with your questions. I will let you know when you've gone too far." Baines said.

Detective Doyle began the interrogation. "Mr. Thornton, were you employed by the man Ethan Rathbone?"

"I had been employed by him for the last thirty-five years."

"On the day of September 17th, did you see Romeo Blanco?"

"Yes, Miss Amora had in the past gone up to Downers Grove to purchase a case of a Filipino delicacy, balut. This particular day she went to his place of business for a different reason."

"This place of business, being The Singapore Sling, an Asian restaurant."

"Yes, she went into the back of the restaurant while I stayed outside of the limousine."

"What happened next?"

"She came out of the door with Mr. Blanco. She instructed me to drive to The Drake Hotel in downtown Chicago."

"What did they do there?"

"They had a long dinner, then came into the back of the limousine. Before Miss Amora got into the backseat, she whispered to me to find an exit close to Milwaukee where there was a wooded area."

"Where you familiar with that area?"

Wesley answered with no hesitation. " I had been there before on her instructions with someone else or others."

"What others?"

Baines interrupted. "Detective, let's stay on the deceased Blanco."

"Can you take us through what happened when you parked the limousine in the woods?"

"After hearing much sounds of sexual activity earlier, these noises turned diabolical. I mean, I could hear Mr. Blanco bearing up under the tearing of his flesh. I got out of the limousine and walked several yards away until Miss Amora now herself, told me it was done."

"What do you mean by she was herself?"

"She turns into a vile creature that can hunt for women's unborn babies or as in Mr. Blanco's case, she wanted to feed on his internal organs."

There was silence. Both detectives looked startled, could not believe what Thornton was saying. Detective Doyle cleared his throat, then continued. "You must know, Sir. This account is getting on the supernatural vein, hard to stomach on many levels."

"I've known about Amora Rathbone's unique problem since she became a teenager. She had been cursed. The explanation and history of this creature she turns into has great strength and great powers of witchcraft and dark magic, coming from the legend of the aswang. Detectives McMahan and Luther Charles have researched the very thing I am talking about."

The younger detective who was standing behind Detective Doyle asked Thornton. "What transpired then? I mean after it was clear Romeo Blanco was dead in the backseat of the limousine?"

"Amora, still in her state of flight to dispose of the victim, I had time to clean the back seat. Instead of throwing away the soiled rags, I put them into the trunk. Amora, herself in human form was busy getting some clothes on I had taken out of the trunk. She didn't notice any soiled rags, out of sight, out of mind."

"Looks like this DNA, you fully meant to show later." Detective Doyle pointed out.

"I made sure when I got Amora back to the estate, she would not notice anything out of order in the backseat. She even mentioned the good job I did with making things look spotless. I knew she would not venture on her own to open the trunk." Wesley said, going on about details of the rags

"My God, man, why on earth would you do such a thing?"

"Master Ethan has for so many months been on the edge for remaining secret about his daughter these many years. I could tell, I needed to be prepared. In the last few weeks, she confessed of taking this experimental drug, Divinia. I believe the side effects were going in reverse and making her more savage." Wesley's bizarre account was defined to possess credibility because of his poise and precise command of the English language.

Forrest Baines spoke up, "Gentleman, I have a signed statement from Clarissa Ross confirming Wesley's alibi on the time Ethan Rathbone was murdered. I believe we have some discussion on bail and his promise not to flee if you want to prosecute him."

Detective Doyle pulled his partner over to the corner of the room. They discussed what they wanted to do next. Detective Doyle approached Mr. Baines. "Well, we will need to go over the limousine, then get Detective McMahan and Detective Charles up here. If you will settle up the bail, you can take him back to Indiana."

"Detectives, I can do you both one better. I drove here in the Rathbone limousine. Mr. Thornton and I will be taking a plane back to Indiana if one of your officers will drive us to O'Hare."

Chapter Twenty-Four
I Have To See Her

I made Grandpa Pete happy by coming to stay in my old room temporarily. Besides, both Luther and I were put on suspension until a full investigation and hearing took place. My grandfather preened his lawyer feathers by getting Luther and I suspension with pay.

The morning sunlight hit me in the face, forcing me to move around in my bed. I looked around the room, my eyes focused on Grace sitting in a rocking chair looking to be knitting. She caught my startled stare. "Well, good morning, Glenda. I'm waiting for you to muster up some consciousness so I can put some ointment on your wounds."

As she approached, I balked back with a scowl on my face, and plenty of bad will towards her. "I'm not some infant with diaper rash. You approaching me with that A&D tube!"

"Sweetie, the skin around your wounds has become painfully tight. To be able to move around without pain this ointment will help." Grace said, undeterred by my growling.

The only part of her nursing that felt uncomfortable was when she lifted off the myriad of bandages. The soft movement of the thick greasy ointment did take away the stinging. Soon, I felt like moving around enough to get out of bed.

"I hate to admit it. You are absolutely right." I said, giving off a sigh of relief.

"I'm going downstairs to prepare breakfast. Come on to the kitchen when you get decent." She said, walking towards my bedroom door.

"Grace, before you go. Why are you doing this?"

She turned around and smiled at me. "You and your partner rid this community of a vile killer. No matter how strange your account sounds, I'm at ease now."

I was again taken by surprise by someone I did not particularly approve of. She would have been the last person I would expect to be in my corner. "Thanks, Grace, for the words and the A&D application."

Getting cleaned up and dressed went rather slow. The skin around my wounds pulled some whenever I moved. The steps going downstairs proved to be the real challenge—with each downward step, my left side sang with stiffness and stabbing prickly soreness.

I walked into the kitchen, finding a welcome surprise. Luther sat at the kitchen table across from Grandpa Pete with most of the top surface covered in file folders and scattered papers.

"Well, this looks like the place to be." I said, showing a cheeriness that was usually not my nature.

Grace brought me a cup of coffee—my first sip pleasantly surprised. She knew how I took it, two sugars and plenty of half n' half. Luther pulled out a file folder underneath a mound of my grandfather's printed papers.

He handed me a file folder. "I've been waiting for you to enter the land of living again."

Drinking my heavenly cup of coffee, I read a report from Ava Mead from the APD Forensics Division. A twinge of excitement hit me as my eyes rested on this statement. "*Bone pieces analyzed came from a young duckling fetus, gestation 22 weeks with non-descript structure density. DNA testing shows the victim, Glenda McMahan was maimed by a large animal where the surface of digits defined a claw configuration.*"

"Luther, did Althea have the same kind of results?" I asked, my mind coming back to a detective's analytical mode of curiosity.

"Yes, indeed. Not totally similar, you had different wounds. The results bear the same message. I'm sure your grandfather will agree with me, this type of confirmation can be used in the trial of Amora Rathbone."

"Pete, can you use this on the brutality charges?" I asked.

"Not directly, only in the explanation of the pursuing of a suspect with unique characteristics of beastly shapeshifting abilities."

"The nature of the way Amora is acting in custody will be difficult to get any kind of information out of her on the attacks and the killings. When she does speak, she repeats over and over that she was beaten before being brought in." Luther said, showing frustration with his crinkled up skin between his eyebrows.

I put down my cup and sat up straight. I said in a loud commanding tone. "I want to see her!" Folded my arms, studying Luther's expression, then looked over at Grandpa Pete.

Grace announced breakfast to be served in the living room. We ate the scrambled eggs, blueberry scones, and bacon in silence until I got a delayed reaction to my loud request.

"I can get you permission to see her at the proper venue. If you promise not to threaten her." Grandpa Pete stressed.

"I can do that. I will do you one better. I want you Pete, Luther and Mitch Gable to watch us from the double-sided glass in the Special Units room at the division." I told him.

In only three days, I was informed by Grandpa Pete I was to be given access to interview Amora. The day of the visitation was to be on the Friday of the same week I got permission. To myself, I named the day, "Bloody Friday". My anticipation was on high alert of how I would siphon from her revealing details to confirm our team's outrageous method of capture.

I took long walks each day in the neighborhood with the family's Great Dane, Lola. My mobility was improving. The neighborhood scenery of palatial homes and rolling manicured lawns gave me the ability to come up with a strategy I had not in mind when I requested this—introduce how she grew up, her parents, including her estranged mother.

The day came. I chose not to wear my usual detective attire of black suit with a white top or dress shirt. I arrived at the detective division wearing jeans and a flowered blouse.

Officer Faraday manned the front desk. He gave forth a startled look. "Wow! You sure look better than the last time we spoke."

"Thanks, Frank. I want to really show my gratitude for your quick thinking. At that time, I was such a mess and not thinking."

"Sergeant Gable gave me the heads up on the prisoner's visitation today. They took her back ten minutes ago. See you later, Glenda." Frank said, with a smile.

Mitch Gable and Luther met me at the door. Mitch said to me. "Your grandfather is on the other side of the glass. She is yours for the next hour."

I walked in, seeing a small brown-skinned woman sitting at the 6 foot rectangular table. She seemed so docile, so frail. Holding still, dressed in inmate orange with her mass of black hair pulled back with a black tie.

I sat down across from her in order to look straight into her eyes with every one of my questions, and every one of her answers. She kept her head down, gazing at her handcuffed wrists. "Amora, do you remember me?"

This question caused her to look up. She stared at me, then spoke. "Your face comes back. It's difficult because you are wearing different kind of clothes today."

"Well, I wanted to make you feel more comfortable. That is why I wore something casual."

"No, you lie. You and your partner have been suspended because you beat me!"

"Amora, we will get back to that very thing. Could you indulge me with some questions about your family?" I changed the subject, struggling to keep my composure staying in a peaceful calm nature.

She nodded.

"That day you first saw me at the Rathbone Estate, I talked about Amado."

"Amado!" She wiggled in her chair, looking down at her wrists again. She looked up and smiled in a sinister manner. "Yes, Amado was my imaginary friend when I was a young girl."

"Why did you have this friend?"

"I was lonely being an only child." She said, her expression changed to one of sadness.

"Why were you so lonely?"

"My mother left when I was thirteen."

"Why did she leave?"

"My mother could not stand me because I told her the attack on our housekeeper was done by Amado."

"Is your mother from the Philippines?"

"Yes, she used to tell me stories of how beautiful her home was on the island of Panay."

"Did she tell you any other stories about her homeland?"

"Yes, but I don't want to tell you! They are very dark stories. One time after I had eaten a balut and threw up, she wept uncontrollably. I was eight at the time, I think." She said, sounding like a child.

"Were you sick for a long time?"

"No, I only got sick once, then begged my mother to play with me."

"Did Amado come up again as you grew up?"

"When I became a teenager during the really hot nights, and a full moon. I would concentrate very hard and made myself be Amado."

"What do you mean by making yourself be Amado?"

"I would get so depressed, a horrible burning took over my mind and body. I would become him and then something else. In the mornings, I would wake up feeling so much better."

I got up. I took off my jeans and got close to where Amora was seated. Automatically she turned to face me. I spoke very carefully, pointing to the left side of my body, "These wounds on my left side came from a winged creature with long claws instead of fingers like you and I have. Do you know what this creature is called?"

She started to shake her head. Her breathing became very shallow. She jumped off her chair and ran to a corner of the room. She pointed at me with her bound hands. "Aswang did that! My mother told me about aswang. You lie again, you tricked me! I didn't want to tell you! Get me out of here!"

While she was cowering and shouting in the corner, Luther came into the room. He came close to Amora, and talked to her like she was a little girl. He was able to get her quieted down. After he took her out of the room, I put my jeans back on.

Mitch Gable and Grandpa Pete came into the room. From looking at the sergeant's face with his blue eyes bulging, I realized I screwed up. "I thought turning her attention to the creature would break her on refusing to own up to all those victims." I went on the defensive.

Mitch bellowed. "Well, you did that! You broke her into hysterics and more brutality in her mind. She won't talk to you again. You are a threat to her now."

"Sarg, I realize showing her my wounds might bring a negative reaction. It could bring some results we can use."

"Well, you did get her to speak about Amado and her mother. That was something." My grandfather said, coming to my defense.

One night at dinner, I heard a very revealing account about Amora. Grandpa Pete told me over my favorite dish, beef stroganoff. "Amora was taken to the Stress Ward at Community Hospital. She was screaming in the middle of the night. Her roommate tried to calm her down. She attacked the roommate by tearing off some of her hair and scratching her face, pretty deep gashes on her forehead and cheeks."

"Do you want me to give you my thoughts?" I asked.

"That's why I brought it up."

"She is slowly getting recall to the horrible things that were done since adolescence. The display of my wounds cracked open recurring images. She is slowly knowing to be true, but instinctively fights against."

Grace voiced a question that made sense. "What can be done now? There has been an arraignment by a public defender, but no trial on the docket as yet."

As I laid in bed that night, I went over my "Bloody Friday" visit. I was so sure showing her my wounds was the right thing to do. When I was in the hospital, Wyla and Luther told me she did not have the usual interrogation because of the discovery of her bruises over most of her upper back. It did not enter my head when all of us had her in our grasp that this case was to be so upside down.

Chapter Twenty-Four
A Funeral

I was alerted by Luther that Wesley Thornton was let go from the Milwaukee authorities and wanted Luther and I to attend Ethan Rathbone's funeral. I took out some dresses I had in storage in Grandpa Pete's attic. Delighted, I pulled out a size 8 black dress still in style which fit me perfectly.

October had only one week left, with temperatures calling for my lightweight lavender jacket to be worn over my dress. I rode with Luther and Althea. She looked stunning in a black jumpsuit showing off her growing baby bump.

The funeral services and burial were to take place in The Crown Hill Cemetery mausoleum. The upper level of the mausoleum was called Peace Chapel featuring the stained glass artistry by way, of the Charles Leonard Merck Family Memorial. Appropriate place for the Rathbone memorial service since he was CEO of IndyMerck founded by Charles Leonard Merck.

We drove through the Gothic Gate entrance off of 38th Street in Indianapolis. "Wow! Some lush and lavish surroundings we have here. Good thing, I dressed up."

The three of us sat through almost ninety minutes of endless eulogies to honor the greatness of a private graceful prince of the wealthy elite in a city that has grown significantly due to Ethan Rathbone's generosity.

Wesley Thornton was the last person to speak at the podium at the raised altar. He seemed to me a changed man. A man of means not the humble devoted butler always dressed in gray pants and a bright red vest. This time he wore a shiny gray suit to match his brilliant blue eyes. He carried himself with full disclosure of culture and sophistication. He used eloquent words to describe what Mr. Rathbone had done for him—an Irish immigrant with only enough money to travel to Indianapolis by bus. Under years of being the Rathbone butler he not only had a wealth of means but became an American citizen.

The audience of over two hundred mourners were instructed to meet downstairs in the corridor of side-by-side crypts close to the South Grounds of the mausoleum. The crowd gathered as Ethan's cherry wood casket was placed into the crypt prepared for such a time as this.

Luther, Althea and I had been instructed to stay in the marble-walled corridor to meet with Wesley. He approached us. "Follow me outside to the summit. We can speak there."

Wesley walked us to the Gothic Chapel where Luther parked his Esplanade. Before we said our mutual goodbyes, he needed to inform us of something quite extraordinary.

"I've decided to give your sergeant full disclosure of the history of how and when Amora became that vile creature that made her your suspect of all those twenty-eight victims." He said with a matter-of-fact tone and no emotion. I wanted to leap and shout, but the atmosphere of the burial of one of the most prominent men in the Indianapolis business world forced me to yell for joy in silence.

In two weeks, the dreaded out of court hearing came. Grandpa Pete told me the hearing was to take place on the third floor of the Government Building with Judge Harker officiating. Inside, I was juggling several emotions—curiosity, fear of the unknown to how much fantastical information Wesley had related to my sergeant, also a nagging dread that Mitch would choose not to divulge one word.

I was to wait in the hallway across from Judge Harker's department offices until Luther was questioned. It would have been nice if I could have stilled my jumping nerves by being able to read one of my recently purchased *Dean Koontz's* thrillers.

I attempted to read the first ten pages, none of the author's brilliant words were sinking in. I was plagued by my preoccupation of *'What the Hell',* was Luther going through in that unnerving police inquisition. I began pacing the long hallway. Halfway down the hall for the tenth time, I heard my grandfather calling my name.

As we reached the door to Judge Harker's private board room, Luther came out giving me a wink. He seemed real together and calm, no wild eyes. I was directed to the head of the long oak table. Grandpa Pete was seated adjacent to me.

Judge Harker, a very distinguished man of color was seated at the other end of the eight-foot table. Mitch Gable sat adjacent to the judge with a female stenographer at the judge's right ready to record every question and every answer. I had known that my grandfather acting as my lawyer was there for moral support only, not to interrupt with objections.

"Madam, state your name and your job description." Judge Harker began the questions.

"My name is Glenda McMahan, detective at the APD detective division."

"How long have you served the city of Anderson?"

"I have served since graduating from the police academy seventeen years ago."

"What spurned you a reasonable and capable officer of the law to embrace this highly speculative type of criminal?"

"With each victim, how they were attacked, their specific injuries, and those professional persons we interviewed coming from the origin of this mysterious legend confirmed time and time again." I wanted to elaborate by naming each person who corroborated with us, but chose to be brief.

Judge Harker was handed a file folder by Mitch Gable. He opened the folder, and held up a report. "I have gone over the report from Sergeant Gable from a lengthy session with Wesley Thornton. I need for you to explain your off-base procedure bringing in the said suspect, Amora Rathbone."

My mouth was so dry, it felt like I had been chewing cotton balls. I took a glass and poured ice water from a pitcher provided. I drank down the entire eight ounces.

"My partner's fiancé has become one of the victims who survived the vicious and savage attack. Althea pressed me at the hospital only a few hours after the attacked happened to see this through no matter how off the grid I had to get."

"So, you used an unlawful practice of brutality to bring her in." The judge stressed, his dark brown eyes stern and menacing.

"Judge, Your Honor, Sir, this suspect was not altogether human when it attacked and murdered its victims. This was definitely from all the information Luther and I compiled the work of a grotesque shapeshifter cursed to perform savage deeds not reasonable to any criminal we had ever encountered before."

The judge seemed to calm down after that last answer. "You mentioned Detective Charles's fiancé. This report details other victims who did not survive. Elaborate the description of the thing before your colleagues strung it up."

"I was walking in the park off of the Cross Street entrance, then captured by a large winged creature. When I was lowered to the ground I saw my captor full face. Reptilian eyes, mouth full of sharp fangs, it spoke to me. With one swipe of its long razor sharp claws, my left side received several deep gashes from my rib cage to my knee."

What I disclosed to Judge Harker defined in the category of 'impossible to believe'. Knowing the judge to be a brilliant legal mind, he needed to witness by my face and audible words I was giving a true account of precisely what the creature did to me.

An officer in patrolman navy blues came into the room. He spoke to Judge Harker first, "Your Honor, I apologize for the interruption. I must speak to Sergeant Gable immediately."

"All right, officer, follow Sergeant Gable and myself to my quarters." The judge raised up from his chair. "Counselor, you and your client remain where you are. We will be back."

I waited until they made their exit. I turned to Grandpa Pete and whispered with an angry hiss. "This is excruciating!"

"My girl, hang in there. Your answers to his tough questions were brilliant and very comprehensible. You didn't shy away from your conviction to this bizarre case. You need to know, Clive Harker is an expert on knowing when someone is telling him what they firmly believe as the truth." Grandpa Pete said, taking my hand.

In what I thought would take hours, Mitch Gable and Judge Harker took to their seats. "Detective McMahan, stand up, please."

I looked at my grandfather. He nodded and motioned for me to stand up. I felt like I had sweat through my suit pants and white shirt.

"I have wanted to explore and weigh the answers from you and your partner further. A serious incident has thwarted my wishes. There seems to be no time to get two other detectives to get up to speed on this twisted upside down case. Due to Mr. Thornton's descriptions that fully confirm your answers this day, it is my duty to reinstate your status as detective. Meet your sergeant and your partner at the detective division to be briefed."

I stood there frozen, thinking, *'what happened? what incident would have rushed this reinstatement?* I watched Judge Harker and Mitch Gable exit out of this board room from a door to the right of where they were seated. Grandpa Pete called to me in a soft tone, "Glenda, Glenda, you can relax. Let's get out of here."

Chapter Twenty-Five

Unaware

Amora made good use of her time in the Stress Ward. She befriended an environmental worker who looked very similar to her—a petite brown-skinned woman with long straight black hair and brown eyes. Arlan came in every morning before lunch to clean her room and bathroom. There was a navy blue patrolman from the APD, 24/7, who guarded outside of Amora's private room.

Arlan, a Filipina dressed in navy blue scrubs went about a certain routine being this particular room housed an inmate from the Women's Unit at the Anderson Jail. She would show her badge to the officer on guard, then knock on the door before entering.

Hearing Amora's voice say, "come in." Arlan would wheel in her cart and ask. "Is it all right to come in and clean?"

Throughout the last week, Amora had learned Arlan was originally from Roxas City and was working on her American citizenship. She had married a man using a long distance connection from the Internet. He was a white man from New Jersey working in Anderson for the last fifteen years owned his own home, and wanted a wife to share his recent good fortune with.

With each day exchanging small talk, Arlan felt comfortable despite the rather alarming circumstances for Amora's reason for being in the

Stress Ward. She went so far as to share with her fellow workers on breaks and at lunchtime how she couldn't understand why this particular patient was tagged, "highly dangerous".

Amora since her confrontation with the other inmate in the jail discovered she possessed magical powers with the ability to control people without touching them. Arlan's routine began in the bathroom to the right of the patient's bed. She picked up a soaked rag with a special solution to sanitize the shower. As Arlan was busy wiping the shower, Amora came up to the back of Arlan very quietly.

Amora waved her hands to the right and to the left inches away from Arlan's head. Arlan dropped the wet rag and turned around. Amora gave forth an odd type of expression. She began to speak in a deep tone with no emotion.

"If you cry out, I have the power to strike you deaf, dumb and blind."

Arlan nodded that she understood. Amora commanded her, "Take off your badge, your scrubs, your underwear. Give them to me."

A naked Arlan handed her what Amora commanded, her mind lost in the full domination of Amora's witchcraft. Amora smiled, saying, "Very good, now I have a question. Are your car keys in one of these pockets?"

Arlan nodded, then pointed to the pants, the right pocket. Amora spoke, "Two more questions, then I will leave without hurting you. Where is your car parked? What is the model of your car? Whisper it to me."

Tears rolled down Arlan's cheeks, but she whispered in Amora's ear. "My car is parked in the employee parking lot behind the main hospital building. It is a Kia Soul."

"Arlan, you have done well. Stay in the shower." Amora said, then she blew into Arlan's face. Arlan collapsed slowly into one of the corners of the shower and closed her eyes.

Amora got dressed, then let her hair hang down like Arlan's was. She adjusted the badge and wheeled the cart out into the corridor. She nodded and smiled at the patrolman who looked up at her seated up against the wall. She showed him her badge, and he waved her on. This badge was of great importance for anyone who worked in the main building and the other buildings at the Community Hospital campus. She left the cart up against a brick wall next to the Emergency Room entrance.

Reaching the employee parking lot, she was able to spot the light green car of belonging to Arlan. Starting the car, she breathed a sigh of relief, then laughed. She was amused to have successfully escaped. Before her main focus of action, she had to make a necessary stop to her office at The Saxony Facility in Noblesville.

Mitch Gable briefed Luther and I as he handed back our badges and our issued hand guns. "The incident is this. Amora Rathbone accosted an environmental worker and escaped from Community." He did not have to tell us to start at the hospital. We made our way to the Environmental Department located in the main hospital building basement.

He had told us to report to the head supervisor on the day shift, a mature robust woman named Thelma. As we made our way through the double doors and down the long dingy painted concrete block hallway, she flagged us down.

We walked into what looked like a break room with two rectangular tables, set of burgundy over stuffed couches, then walked into the supervisors office equipped with three desks for each shift supervisor. Thelma directed us to where Arlan was seated. "Detectives, this is Arlan. Close the door behind you. These heifers are gossip hounds if they come waltzing into the break room before they are supposed to."

I questioned Arlan first, "Hello, I'm Detective McMahan. What did she do to you?"

"I was wiping down the shower in the bathroom. She came to me from behind. We're the same height, so I looked into her eyes. Something in her stare and the sound of her voice made me think of the island's handed-down legend. I was terrified. She commanded me to hand over to her my scrubs, underwear, and my car keys."

"Did she threatened or touch you?"

"She did not touch me at all. Her threat was if I cried out, she had the power to strike me deaf, dumb and blind. I believed her because of the legend I mentioned. You probably think I'm crazy." Arlan began to cry.

Her mouth quivered. "Hearing about what someone cursed, turning into something so evil and grotesque! She was not turned, still in human form. I know somehow I was face to face with the ancient evil I was told as a young girl."

"Arlan, not in any way do we think you are crazy. Both of us have a large amount of knowledge of this legend." I reassured her.

Luther spoke up, "Did this patient know you had knowledge of this legend?"

"The only thing I told her was that I am originally from Roxas City. We did not have any conversation of Filipino superstitions."

Luther and I looked at each other. I sat there telling myself, *'How is this possible? I saw the black duckling fetus burn.'*

Luther probed more, "Did she turn into some horrible looking creature?"

"No, she remained human like you and me. One thing, one morning she mentioned how she and I looked so much alike. We could have been twins. There was something in her eyes, the color deep red." Arlan said, shaking all over. Holding on to the crumpled tissue as if it was some prized possession.

Luther told Arlan. "Arlan, you have been very helpful. With the history of this type of criminal, she has a specific agenda in mind. She will not come for you. I'm certain of it. I am giving you my card. Give me a call if you have any concerns or fears."

"What about my car. I need it!" Arlan insisted.

"We will alert those here in Anderson, and other areas even to Indianapolis about your car. Describe it, make and model."

"It is a 2014 light green Kia Soul."

When we got to Luther's vehicle, I told him. "We need to warn Wesley."

"First, let me call Luana Barba. Hang tight."

I sat there feeling a rushing panic all through me. Now that I had been reinstated, I needed to stay cool and calm. Getting hysterical would not help in this tense situation. I stared at Luther's expression. He not only reached Luana but received something we could act on.

He placed his cellphone in his console and turned to me. "Luana said her powers of controlling people live on in her. Although she did lose her ability to shapeshift. Then she told me something very interesting. A month ago she had sent a mixture in pill form of the drug Divinia and ground up cassava root to Wesley. If she ingests this by mouth or put into her food or drink, she will die."

My mind raced. This combination of a lethal potion would have to be a last effort. This type of solution could backfire on us and bring us both to be prosecuted as murderers despite her being the most evil creature on the planet. On the other side of the coin, we bring her back to custody she would surely escape again.

Luther called Wesley. "Oh good, I got you. Are you alone at the house?" Luther nodded up and down. "Good, Amora has escaped from Community Hospital. She could be on her way to you. Glenda and I are on our way to where you are."

Now on the road to the Rathbone estate, I called the division. "Hey, Officer Faraday, it's Glenda. Could you put out an APB on a stolen car, owner Arlan Gomez, a 2014 light green Kia Soul? Thanks, Frank, you're a prince."

I was conflicted and confused on how I was looking at this new development. I felt clueless as to how we would overtake a suspect with witchlike powers. At the same time, this was the most alive I had felt since collapsing on the division floor after Amora had been say, de-aswanged. I was beginning to believe what Wyla said in the hospital about saying goodbye to living a normal life after rubbing up to the supernatural.

Chapter Twenty-Six

Synchronized Suspense

It was getting close to four p.m., Clarissa Ross had finished filing a stack of results from a three-month testing symposium in the St.Paul/Minneapolis area. She received an email from Amora Rathbone's regional director— Ms. Rathbone did not show up, I went on without her. I tried reaching her several times, but got no response.

The phone rang. She picked it up, "Clarissa, this is Wesley. You might get a visit from Amora. Do not let her get into her office. If she comes through, press the button under your desk for security."

Sounding confused and somewhat panicked, she asked, "Why are you so insistent on security?"

"She escaped from the Stress Ward at Community Hospital in Anderson. She's dangerous, Clarissa. It's official on her being the suspect of those 28 victims. Call me when security has her under custody." Wesley said, laying out his insistence for Clarissa to be on the alert.

When Clarissa hung up, Amora showed up a few paces from the secretary's desk. Clarissa's heart rate accelerated as she was overcome by intense fear. Quick thinking, she decided to treat Amora with warmth and a declaration of missing her.

"Ms. Rathbone, I'm so pleased you are free from police custody. I'm surprised you're here. Are those clothes the one you wore in the jail?"

"You could say that. I'm here to retrieve some important items in my office." Amora answered Clarissa with an odd stare.

Clarissa stood up. "I can't let you go in your office right now. I'm sorry, Amora."

Amora moved in closer to Clarissa's right side profile. Her secretary bent over to press the button to alert security. In a flashing movement, impossible to see with the naked eye. Amora took ahold of the sharp letter opener beside the desk computer monitor. With incredible force, Amora sliced Clarissa's neck from ear to ear.

She raced into her office still holding on to the bloodied letter opener. She got into her middle drawer on her desk to retrieve her car keys and a small purse. She failed to think about the bloodied marks she had made on the drawer.

Running out into the hallway outside of the research department, she was met with two uniformed guards. One of them asked her. "Ms. Rathbone, we received a red alert. What's going on?"

The other guard got sight of the bloodied letter opener. "Ma'ham, you better come with us."

Amora pointed the letter opener to both of the guards with a command. "You will let me pass in order not to be in grave peril for your lives!"

They stood there frozen—not able to respond or move forward in any way. She smiled at their trancelike faces, as she passed them. Both guards were caught up within a warped state, unable to think on their own or move. She was amused by the power she had over people's minds enough so they could not move or speak. She was energized by the newfound power she possessed.

Wesley Thornton instead of choosing to be on the alert for a possible visit from Amora, began preparing a gourmet dinner—red aspic and an entrée of breaded sweetbreads. As he finished preparing the aspic—a red jellied mixture of ground up chicken livers in the form of a bundt cake. Amora entered the large kitchen.

He heard her breathless voice. "I have a bone to pick with you and my father!"

He dared not to look into her face. With his back to her, he placed the perfectly set aspic in her direct gaze. "My sweet girl, while you were gone. I was on a perpetual vigil at Methodist Hospital. Your father suffered a stroke. I wasn't aware where you were. I was so preoccupied with Master Ethan's condition."

"Is he all right?"

"He made it over the hump. He still can't speak. The doctor is hopeful with his vital stronger every day. I thought I would celebrate his coming out of the coma by preparing a gourmet favorite. And here you are to enjoy the dinner with me!" Wesley said in a soft controlled tone. He put the pig pancreas on the island counter to begin breading it.

Amora stood there attempting to read his mind and his mood. His mind was preoccupied with a fond memory. She was unable to get anything of a negative nature from his thoughts. She sighed, and said. "Looks like you've picked my favorites. Come to think of it, I'm starving!"

"You go to your quarters and freshen up. I will ring the bell when dinner is to be served." Wesley said, glancing her way with a congenial smile.

She took him up on his suggestion, feeling not a bit of animosity towards him. Entering her elegant bedroom, she felt secure and content for the first time since she had been taken into custody. What brought the most pleasure was a hot bubbly bath in her green and cream marble tub. As the hot scented water of strawberries and cream pouring gently over her shoulders and supple breasts, she entertained thoughts of how she could work to bring good relations back with her father.

She breathed in the lingering aroma of the delicious preparations of the sweetbreads filtering up from the kitchen to the stone staircase. She coiled her long thick black hair into an attractive sizable bun on the crown of her head. She dressed in one of her long flowing silk lounging robes.

Hearing the dinner bell, she waltzed down the Tower staircase resembling a stunning lady of great prestige—not a cold-blooded killer who forty-five minutes ago sliced her secretary's throat. Wesley Thornton stood at the base of the staircase feeling conflicted—viewing such a vision of beauty would be a waste with her end coming so soon.

"Oh, before I forget, Wesley. You need to see about heating my Tower quarters as cold weather approaches."

"By all means, I will get right on that."

They took their seats at the elegantly decorated dining room table. Amora sat down admiring her appetizer of the red aspic in a large goblet, and the aromatic four-piece breaded sweetbreads smelling of herbs and butter. Wesley sat down at the opposite end of the cherry wood table. This gave Amora the signal to begin.

Wesley ate his appetizer as well, only he chose to serve himself a tossed salad. Amora was enjoying her aspic so much she looked like a she had not eaten in days. The well prepared appetizer was so far afield of what she had to endure being in the Women's Ward in the Anderson Jail.

She drank down a glass of wine, then moved on to the sweetbreads. She spoke up after realizing there was only two bites left of her entrée. "Forgive me, Wesley. I guess I missed good food so much, I lost myself in your expert preparation.

In a matter of five minutes, she stopped eating. Her eyes were filled with puzzlement, then she put her hands onto her stomach. Wesley looked up from his salad. "Miss Amora, is there something wrong? You look like you're in pain."

"What did you put in my food? I feel like I've eaten glass!" She shouted, struggling to get up from her seat.

All she wanted to do was make it to the end of the table and reach for Wesley's neck. Her forward movement could be compared to someone trying to walk with weights attached to their ankles.

"Miss Amora, I lied about Master Ethan. When you had shapeshifted into your vile manifestation, you captured him and killed him by tearing your own father to pieces!" Wesley shouted out with self-satisfaction on his face.

He stood up. "This is justice. You would have done a world of harm to anyone who would have crossed your path."

She reached for his throat, but her body could not stand any longer. As she descended in agony, her mind was fully active in a mode of revenge. Her mouth and teeth clamped onto Wesley's left hand. He jerked and forced her off his hand. She collapsed onto the antique white carpet.

Last bit of movement, her body jerked with a large amount of blood oozing out from her nose and mouth onto the antique white carpet. Wesley watched her contorted convulsing messy end, going over in his mind what Luana Barba told him—*before the sun comes up, dismember her, bury the parts overnight. In the morning light, dig them up, and incinerate the body parts.*

He sighed, then sobbed for a few moments. Not from the pain of her bite, but he was overcome by the death of such a beautiful woman— the waste of it all. He was there when she began her formative years. Before the legend started to surface, she was a beautiful quiet child. Her innocence during those years made her kind to all those she came in contact with.

How could he eliminate a child he remembered to be quite extraordinary? He shook his head in an instant his whole mood changed. He took a white cloth napkin and wrapped his hand until he could clean and bandage it.

He went over to the dining room windows to see if the gardener Luis was still busy racking leaves around the front lawn circle. He had time to retrieve a tarp out of the backyard shed, then roll Amora's body into the tarp, take it to the greenhouse. He knew Luis would be coming to the end of his work for the day. So much to do in so little time.

As Wesley walked to the shed, Luis waved him down. "Senore, do you need me tomorrow?"

Wesley yelled. "No, Luis, you can take the whole weekend off."

Watching Luis walk towards the three-car garage, Wesley began his synchronized plan going over in his mind—*get the tarp, roll her and get the covered body into the greenhouse. I have to get rid of my clothes, burn them and get back into the house to begin cleaning up the blood, her quarters and the kitchen. I have to do this by the time the detectives get here.*

Luis had remembered to tell the butler one more thing before he got into his truck. He came walking around the front of the house to catch a naked butler put his clothes into the rusted steel drum next to the backyard shed. Luis stopped and hide behind a bush until Wesley had walked back into the back of the house. He didn't want the butler to see him due to the uneasy feeling he possessed seeing the butler naked burning a wad of clothing in the yard drum for some unknown reason.

Wesley cleaned his wound where he could see deep holes shaped like an open mouth. He used some antiseptic and wrapped it tight with gauze to stop the bleeding. His next move to make a fast attempt to clean the blood from the dining room carpet. It was not totally gone, but would have to do. He cleared off the table, then ran up the stone staircase to take away any evidence of Amora being in the house. The stinging pricks of pain reminded him of Amora's vengeful last act.

He had no time to worry about his hand now, he heard the buzzer. He knew the detectives were at the gate.

Chapter Twenty-Seven

The Show Must Go On

My mind raced with fighting uncertainties invading my stress threshold. Questions of "what if" almost brought me to a tempting bout of screaming. A situation on the I69 approaching the Binford Avenue sign into downtown Indianapolis caused me to actually act out what was going on inside my head, *what the Hell!*

Luther had to decrease his speed to twenty-five miles per hour as the five o'clock traffic compounded to an eventual halt. "We're not going anywhere for a while. I'm coming up with the idea, Amora decided to get out of Indiana. She's got thousands of dollars at her fingertips." Luther said, trying to cater to my reasonable side.

I felt strongly before she might leave the state—she definitely had unfinished business to tend to with Wesley. From going over and over in my mind the details we received from the environmental worker—not only did she realize her powers of controlling people was evident, but her recall of those who could bring a full verdict of guilty rested on the person of Wesley Thornton.

Almost two hours later, we drove up the pristine drive to the gate intercom. Luther pressed it. A familiar voice. "Who goes there?" Luther looked over at me. "See, he sounds alive to me."

"Wesley, it's Detective Charles." In two minutes, the gate opened.

I looked at Luther as we waited at the front door. "Well, can't help being crazed. This has been one damn thing after another today!"

Right from opening the heavy double doors, and letting us into the grand foyer, I could tell Wesley was not his cool-as-a-cucumber self. I spoke up, "Wesley, you look a bit harried, all out of sorts."

"I've been busy preparing a difficult gourmet dinner with Forrest Baines, Master Ethan's lawyer. We had some legal matters to discuss. Come into the kitchen. You can visit while I clean it up." Wesley said, then tuned around before we got into the kitchen. "Do you two care for an espresso?"

Luther chimed in with enthusiasm. "We would be crazy to turn down your espresso."

We sat down at the kitchen small square table. Wesley prepared the espresso, then busied himself by cleaning up the dinner mess and filling up the dishwasher with dirty dishes and pots and pans.

I began a lengthy discussion to prompt any rise of emotion from our busy butler, "I was racked with worry the whole time we had to wait for the traffic jam to clear. To me it took hours and a day. You didn't get an unpleasant visit from our escaped criminal?"

He would not meet my stare, then seemed cavalier in giving me a response. "She didn't show up here. As we ate our dinner, Forrest was told about her escape. He was pleased with the food, but couldn't get out of here fast enough."

He didn't miss a beat as he poured the espresso into two demitasse cups and handed one to me and one to Luther. Luther noticed his bandaged hand. "What happened to your hand?"

"Oh, I was in such a hurry to prepare dinner, I slipped with the knife as I was cutting up the chicken livers." Wesley said, acting like the injured hand was nothing. He looked over at my face, to see I was not buying the story. He changed the subject and asked me a question, "Detective McMahan, while your prisoner was in custody. Did Amora know her father was dead?"

"No, I wanted to tell her when seeing her after I got out of the hospital. My questions for her turned another direction. She got hostile when I introduced any knowledge of the legend of aswang." I said, taking the demi-tasse cup to my lips.

Luther asked Wesley. "Where do you think she is going to land?"

"You know. I've had this thought all day. She could be going overseas to the Philippines to look for her mother. I know she is confused, but I believe she will realize her father is gone. Luana Barba in conversation over the phone related to me those that had lost the chick by being beaten as your group had done. Slowly thoughts and images come back of what she had turned into."

We finished our espresso. I felt Wesley was hiding something but held off on drilling him. Luther possessed that goofy look of—we are good here, let's move on. We said our goodbyes and thanked him for his hospitality.

The sky gave its evening display of the brightness of the sun meeting the horizon line with the commencing of dark blue and purple clock of night closing in. My instincts kept nagging me as we made our way back to Anderson.

"You know, Luther. Things in that house seemed odd. When we all walked through the dining room to get to the grand foyer. I spotted a pinkish large spot on the carpet close to the chair at the head of the table in the dining room. Wesley's coloring looked real flushed like he had been moving a piano or something like dead weight."

"Glenda, I know you are super excited about being reinstated. Don't make something out of nothing. That spot on the dining room carpet could be anything." Luther said, attempting to downplay my hunches.

The night brought with it a weariness and a desire to go back to Grandpa Pete's, curl up on his living room sectional and read. We had to check in with our sergeant. Coming up with nothing, I dreaded his ugly temper, shooting rays of utter disappointment our way.

Our sergeant was at the open door to his office. When he spotted us, he yelled. "Get over here, now!"

We filed in, both of us knowing Mitch Gable demanded clear-cut answers, not excuses. He sat down, turning his swivel chair in the direction, viewing his profile. "Well, what do you have for me?"

Luther was brave enough to give him a summary. "We questioned the environmental worker who Amora accosted. She told us Amora threatened her to the point she thought she would lose her life."

"Here we go, some more supernatural crap!"

I spoke up. "Sarg, what we learned from the worker, then went on to the Rathbone estate, Amora is getting her witchlike powers back in strength. She will not shapeshift ever again. Putting it into a nutshell. Wesley Thornton wasn't much help. Luther and I came to the conclusion she has made arrangements to get out of Indiana, and go off to where her mother lives in the Philippines."

Gable jumped out of his chair. "So, not only have we lost a dangerous criminal, but she has moved on to parts unknown overseas! Do you two know how this department will look when the press gets wind of her missing?"

He held his head down for a few minutes then looked at me. "Glenda, do you believe Thornton?"

"No, Sarg, not a word. He's hiding something."

"And Luther, what say you?"

"So much is up in the air. Wesley did mention about her mother. I can get on the computer and start searching for Divinia Rathbone." Luther said.

"Tell you what, the both of you. Go to your respective homes and get adequate rest. For now, this case is closed, no prisoner, no trial." The sergeant said in a calming tone.

"Sarg, give us more time! I know we can find more if we go back to the Rathbone estate." I pleaded.

"Glenda, you are going to have to do that on your own time. We have to show this community, business as usual. I'll see you both back here on Monday morning." Mitch Gable said, giving me an expression I better not push.

Chapter Twenty-Eight

Is It Business As Usual?

Sergeant Gable threw a stack of cases at Luther and I. Again, this community was plagued by growing meth labs. We went through a particular report on a suspected location in a fairly safe neighborhood called Meadowbrook on the south end of the city off of South Main Street. We began surveillance on a quiet street called Elva.

I parked my vintage car across the street, almost to the end of the street from a known trafficked small house three houses up from our parked car. I felt my car would be best to use since it looked like it would be owned by an older person with a love of custom vehicles.

On the nights when there was very little goings on in or out of the house, I would try to call Wesley Thornton. I did not receive any reply after calling myriad times a day.

Around five p.m., Luther popped his head around my cubicle wall. "Hey, remember those Indy detectives we met during Rathbone's autopsy?"

"I sure do."

"They are at the front desk. They need to see us."

Detective Felts and Detective Lutz were studying the recent, "Wanted" posters on the large bulletin board across from the high counter. I noticed their eyes were peeled on the poster of Amora Rathbone.

Detective Felts turned around as we approached them. "This poster is quite coincidental. We are here to match up fingerprints from this missing prisoner."

My keen mind on this escaped woman was going through excitement cartwheels. I came up with an answer before there was any kind of comparison. "I bet she is mixed up in a homicide."

Detective Lutz seemed amused, but attempted to get serious. "Ms. Rathbone's secretary had her throat cut last week. We think the fingerprints we found in Ms. Rathbone's office desk and the murder weapon found in the back staircase down from the research offices need confirmation you two can help us with."

Luther spoke up. "Detectives, follow us to my computer. I can pull up Amora Rathbone's prints."

Like a group of college students waiting for their final exam scores, the Indy detectives, Luther and I stood by in bated breath as Luther printed the fingerprint findings. He handed the result to Detective Felts.

He compared a copy of her fingerprints to the copy of their analyzed prints. "I'm glad we drove through the 5 o'clock I69 hellish traffic. They are a match!"

I spoke up, "That day Luther and I got the word of her escape we visited Wesley Thornton. To me, he didn't seem like himself. I've called him several times, and no answer."

"Well, we will give Mr. Thornton a visit." Detective Lutz assured me.

I wanted so badly to volunteer to join them, but Luther glared at in such a way I knew not to go there. It did feel reassured that my instincts were still working very well.

With each day on our super boring snail's pace surveillance, I could not contain myself until Sunday. Luther and I negotiated with the sergeant to give us a break. Luther used his sure-fire excuse of Althea threatening to divorce him if he didn't get a day off soon.

There did come a break in our recent case one Saturday night very late. From the house we had been casing, twelve different types of vehicles parked in front only stayed on average ten minutes. The ages ranging of the visitors looked to be around twenty to thirty, mostly males. I knew it was only a matter of time, there would be some kind of altercation with a surety—Saturday night would be the point in time of a bust to take place.

Sunday came. I shuffled out of bed around one p.m. My first thought was a strong cup of coffee. Grace was busy on what Grandpa Pete called "supper"—a traditional late afternoon full course meal which farmers in the Midwest had established a hundred years or so to get into bed early to rest before their rising, before the crack of dawn.

I poured what was left in the coffeemaker, doctored it up to my liking, then proceeded for my getting-ready protocol upstairs. Grace shouted before I left the kitchen, "Glenda, you have that expression of leaving-for-the-day. We are having beef and noodles!"

I peeked my head back through the archway molding. "And I know it will be delicious. Leave me a plate, Grace. I've got a huge lead on a case."

Walking to my vintage 1988 baby blue Camaro, I spied Luther arms folded leaning against the passenger side. "Do you think I was going to let you spy around the Rathbone Estate by yourself?"

"I'll unlock the car. I thought you were going to spend your day off with Althea?"

He got in, "Nope! She's in Louisville at her sister's home."

As we got to 38th Street, travelling to North Meridian, Luther got curious. "What if Thornton refuses to let us in?"

"We will park in that open lot past the Rathbone natural wall of poplar trees. I'm glad you dressed casual. We will be doing some climbing."

"Oh, you've done this before, I assume."

"Wyla and I broke in when you were on leave."

After parking and locking my car, we passed the natural barrier. A tan colored picket fence divided the Rathbone acreage to the neighbor's south lawn. The top of the spikes came up to Luther's eye level.

"You climb on top of my shoulders and jump off into the open lawn." Luther instructed.

I did not like his strategy, but I was clueless on a better idea to get to the other side of this fence. It was the jumping I dreaded. Luther said. "Don't think about how you will land. Like tearing off a bandage, do it quick!"

I did it with not even the twist of an ankle. Thankful my hips and legs were elastic enough not to break any bones. I was amazed as Luther used a long branch to pole jump over the fence.

We made our way towards the house passing the three-car garage. I stopped. Luther asked, seemed puzzled why I stopped. "What are you thinking?"

"I want to peek into each window. What could it hurt?"

We looked into each window. In the third window, we saw a car. Luther shouted out the model and make immediately, "That's a Toyota Camry, looks to be a 2015 or 2016."

I wrote the identity of the car into my pocket-size notebook out of my back jean pocket. We moved on to the front door. I rang the doorbell several times. We stood there for another ten minutes, nothing. A voice came from behind us, deep with a noticeable accent, "What do you want?"

Luther and I jumped almost a foot, then turned around to see a stout brown-skinned dark haired man holding a rake. I explained. "Sir, we had an appointment with Wesley Thornton. There was no response from the gate, so we walked into the lawn. We are detectives from Anderson Police Department."

His expression read surprise. "That explains how you made it from the mile long natural barrier!"

"Forgive me, but. Who are you?" I sheepishly inquired.

"I'm Luis, the Rathbone gardener. Mr. Wesley has gone on a trip. When he put this place for sale, he told me he was going to look for somewhere more peaceful than here. He needed to get away."

Luther got closer to the gardener. "Could help us with something? Have there been strange things to happen before Mr. Thornton left?"

"Like, seeing Mr. Wesley walking from the backyard shed to the back of the house naked. Is that strange enough?" Luis answered.

I asked, "When was that?"

"It was two weeks ago on a Friday night."

"Another question and we will let you get back to work. Whose car is that in the garage?" I asked, hoping Luis would not lose patience with our lingering presence.

"That car is Missy Amora's. I thought working these days on the front part of the lawn I would run into her. I haven't seen her at all. That same night I saw Mr. Wesley naked, I had to get something out of the garage. There her car was parked next to the Rathbone limousine." Luis said, then turned to get back onto his small riding cart.

Chapter Twenty-Nine

Going On Leave

One cold November night, Luther and I were sitting in my car on our surveillance duty. Three guys in hoodies walked out of the residence we were watching. The porch light came on with a woman, slender with an enormous trail of thick pink and blonde streaked hair shouting from the open door.

What ensued after her incessant cries brought both of us out of the car. Luther whispered, "Don't run until we see fists landing."

Two of the guys in the front of the emaciated man the woman called Lance, yelled. "You guys shorted us!"

The youths looking to be younger than Lance, in a matter of seconds had him on the ground plowing one blow after another on his head, back, and stomach. That was our cue. With handguns pointed we were on the ruckus in ten seconds.

I pulled out my badge and yelled out. "Stop! We are the police!"

Luther held his gun only two paces from the out-of-breath youths. Lance got up and began moving towards the front door. "Freeze, don't move one more step!" I shouted. Holding him steady, I called for backup.

Luther had put both of the youths in handcuffs and read them their rights. I had Lance in handcuffs, read his rights to him. We approached

Luther's prisoners. I asked the youths, "What was the reason for kicking the guy's ass?"

One of them stood there shaking all over and having trouble catching his breath, he spoke shivering. "Oh, what the hell! The guy got greedy, his chick, too. We gave them what was agreed on the phone before we got over here."

I laughed at them. I was amused by their cavalier attitude about being caught. "Just curious. Didn't you two happen to find a baby blue older car with a couple of people sitting in the front seat only two houses from this one rather odd."

"We're too fucked up most of the time to notice shit!" The other one said.

With that sterling confession of high intelligence, two squad cars pulled up. Four officers from the APD came walking up to Luther. "Well, Detective Charles, what do we have here?" One of the taller officers asked.

"These fine gentlemen bought product from our boy Lance here being held by Detective McMahan. They have had their rights read to them. You officers take them off our hands, and we will give a look-see into the house." Luther instructed.

We walked into the home where the woman with the mass of hair was holding a young girl. I assumed to be her daughter. "She is my daughter. Don't take me in, both my parents are out of town."

Luther walked into the kitchen while I dealt with her. "It depends if we find something in your kitchen. You will have to make arrangements with someone in order for us to take you into the division for some questions." I said, speaking without rancor.

Luther came out with a long rectangular baking pan. "Ma'ham, what was in this pan?"

She put her head down and sobbed. She walked her daughter over to the couch, "Sweetie, sit down. Mommy needs to talk to these officers."

"This is what Lance had sold to those guys. We've been cooking meth and processing it for a while." She told us, then sobbed again. "Now, I know they are going to take my daughter away from us."

I got closer to her, and lifted up her chin. "Miss, you knew full well what you were doing. Call a friend, or some relative to pick up your daughter. We will wait while you pack her up and she is picked up." This was one of the worst scenarios about any bust—when a young child appeared on the scene. The look on the little girl's face of sheer fear to be taken from her mother, that was a disparity I would save back in my personal vault of regrets.

This stake out was fairly speedy, some can last for months. I believe the nature of the quietness of the street worked in our favor. Most of the other residents were older—left for work, or to the grocery then came home and stayed until their routine started the next day. This bust was over in time for Thanksgiving.

Thanksgiving at Grandpa Pete's came with it, a well-rounded table of holiday participants to enjoy the amazing turkey dinner Grace had so aptly prepared. Luther and Althea joined us which was a delightful perk to the day. My appetite was sated. I enjoyed the company for a time, but my mind became overwhelmed with nagging questions about why Wesley Thornton left Indiana so quickly. His departure almost overrode my burning desire to find Amora even knowing I put my body and soul in extreme peril.

Luther and Grandpa Pete were enjoying a carafe of Pinot Grigio while Althea helped Grace in the cleaning up of the dining room and the kitchen. I approached the men reclining in my grandfather's study. "Grandpa Pete, I need to steal Luther away for a moment."

"Oh, Glenda, can't you stop the detective work for Thanksgiving?" Grandpa Pete lamented.

"You know I'm not programmed that way. It's important."

We went to a corner of the living room where the grand piano sat. Luther sat down on the piano bench. His eyebrows raised. "What's up?"

"I'm going to pay the Rathbone attorney a visit to find out where Wesley went. Do you want to join me?"

"Of course, I assume we'll be headed to Indy first thing Monday."

I smiled and bowed my head, "I appreciate your acceptance without my cajoling."

Luther got up. He put his arm around me. "Now, join your grandfather and me for a drink. Partner, you need to loosen up."

Forrest Baines office appeared as elegant as his former client. The secretary did not hesitate after we gave our usual official introduction. "You are fortunate, detectives. Mr. Baines is not with a client. I'll ring him before you go in."

We walked into his office, walls made up of Maplewood siding with each stick of furniture resembling the fancy drawing room of an English lord. A tall white-haired man in a charcoal gray suit stood looking out his office windows.

Luther announced. "Mr. Baines, you're very gracious to see us in a cold call, such as it is."

He turned around, appearing unaffected but gracious in a forced way, "I was expecting you, detectives. State your request."

"I've been trying to reach Wesley for weeks. Found out from the Rathbone gardener, he's left Indiana, and put the estate up for sale." I summed up what we knew so far.

"Detective McMahan, you realize, I hope. The reason for Mr. Thornton's departure is grief. He lost his friend and employer in such a grisly way. He needed to go somewhere nothing like here for peace and tranquility." The attorney stared at me pressing the matter of Wesley's emotions.

Luther walked closer, nose to nose with Mr. Baines. "We have an escaped prisoner, highly dangerous. As you well know, Wesley cooperated with the Wisconsin and Indianapolis authorities about Amora's crimes. He is still in danger even though he's thousands of miles from here."

Baines nodded, then sat down behind his massive ornately carved desk. "Well, my compliments, Detective Charles. You have a solid argument. Wesley Thornton became sole heir to the ample Rathbone estate. The night Ethan went missing, I received an email from him to change his will. Wesley has the funds to go anywhere in the world. From a call I received last week, he purchased a home in Central California."

"Can you be more specific on the location?" I asked.

"Yes, the most breathtakingly beautiful place I've known to have experienced, Big Sur. I don't have the precise address of the new residence." Baines said, then stood up. A noticeable gesture he wanted us to leave. We compiled with his silent request.

During the drive back to Anderson, I garnered my tenacious nature to share with Luther. "This sounds a bit nutty, but I'm going to Big Sur. We need to know a lot of loose ends only Wesley can provide."

Luther held back on his response during our entire commute. This course of action on his part, he knew always drove me "up a wall". I kept looking over at my partner, trying to read his stone-cold face. I huffed and lamented inwardly until he eventually opened up.

In the police department's parking lot, Luther turned off his Esplanade. He turned to me with remorse in his large dark eyes. "I know you're determined to do this. Althea told me last night her gynecologist found dangerous stress to her liver. As the baby grows with each coming month, she will be forced to practice bed rest. That was the reason she went to visit her sister today."

"So, you're telling me, you can't join me on my decision." I said, in noticeable disappointment.

His large dark eyes blinked slowly, he confessed. "As usual you read me right. I have to stay here to be on call for Althea."

I did not answer back. Not of the mind and reality of being committed to someone else, I wrestled inwardly to fully understand Luther's plight. I felt a bit of self-loathing on my present state of not being committed to anyone.

We went back to the division, dealing with final reports of the Elva Street bust. I got up with my finished report in hand, heading to Mitch Gable's office.

I knocked. He yelled on the other side of the glass door. "Enter, if you have to!"

He looked over from his computer screen, "Great, detective, the chief just called about that particular bust."

"Yeah. Sarg, I've got some time saved up, almost three weeks. I'm wanting to a leave. Already told Luther. He's staying here."

"Thank God for that! I can't have both of you MIA! Knowing you, it's not for pleasure." The sergeant peeked at me from his glasses planted on the bridge of his nose.

I walked towards the door, from my back I heard him say. "Come back in one piece and don't let your brain power be muddied up by what you find. I'll need you in good shape for work when you get back."

A small portion of my former comfort zone here in Madison County could have made me turn to my sergeant saying I had changed my mind on this trip. It was too late. I was fully committed to going, no matter how strange the road turned out to be.

Chapter Thirty

Bungalow By The Sea

A real estate agent in Carmel, California showed her client the last entry of the day. It was around the time where the sunsets were at their most colorful in the wealthy community of Big Sur. A redwood dominated home in the heart of the mountainous region off of Highway 1 forced Wesley Thornton to breathe a heavy sigh contained in appreciation for what was before him and around his field of vision.

"This combination style of California Bungalow and Victorian Shingle will give you a private view of a redwood canyon, making way for the active ocean waves crashing into large rock formations. The main house possesses multi-level open bean ceilings." The statuesque blonde with a mass of loosely-curled hair told Wesley. She waltzed him around the spacious terrace that gave him the spectacular view.

His eyes went beyond the railing of the terrace to see a weathered door in front of a rounded dark rock down below. "That's odd." Wesley commented.

The real estate agent moved up beside him. "Oh, Yes. The previous owner had that door chiseled into the rock. With the coolness inside this type of cave, he used the interior for his photography."

"Tell you what. This is the most promising residence you've shown me yet. I'm of the mind to pay your entire sale price. Is that something we can agree to?" Wesley stated with his most charming smile.

The agent was almost speechless. She cleared her throat. "Why, this is quite extraordinary! Yes, I will even take off a couple of thousand for you."

"Madame, I will give you my attorney's contact information in Indiana. He can send the amount to you in any way you two agree to. This house will definitely work well for me." Wesley said.

Now that Wesley was set on where he would put up stakes in Big Sur, he purchased the most expensive dry red wine in Carmel. He took two sips, the rich taste of the vintage failed to satisfy the rumbling in his stomach, and the burning in his chest. In the last few weeks, he found most food caused a nagging ache to linger in his stomach until the next day. One night he could not stand the pain until he was compelled to eat a package of raw chicken livers. The pain went away, and he felt satisfied.

After consuming raw calf's liver from the gourmet shop in Carmel, he thought about the moment when Amora bit his left hand. The day after he buried her body parts, the markings from her bite had disappeared. In the back of his mind, he entertained dark thoughts of a dread he fought against—she cursed him with that last action before she breathed her last.

He knew inside his lot was to be transformed into some king of ghoul, hungering for something most mortals find utterly repulsive. Living with the Rathbones and knowing this legend first hand—he had become an avid student of Philippine Lower Mythology.

This night of knowing he was to move into his new home, he wasn't thinking of the excitement of making the home his own. His thoughts rested on how to find a human specimen to satisfy his worsened state of unmentionable cravings for human internal organs and human flesh. A most depraved state for a man once prided himself on elegant decorum of the most delicious forms of fine dining where the food was cooked, and not of the raw nature or of the humankind cannibalism.

Days of the moving came where he had purchased a bedroom set, a sectional, many bookshelves for his many books shipped in from

Indianapolis, and another set of metal shelves he was to use for the seaside cave down below his home.

His mind was taken in to the usefulness all around, as he examined the inside of the cave. It was the size of his modest quarters in the Rathbone Estate. The walls were solid rock with a faint odor of the sea waters. He knew this space would work due to the coolness, almost the feel of a thirty-degree temperature sure to keep someone's body parts fresh for days or more. The metal shelves he brought in would store the body parts and inner organs placed in transparent heavy plastic to ensure freshness for his challenged palette.

I was packing for my drive West as Grandpa Pete entered my bedroom. His gray blue eyes seemed sullen. "Glenda, do you have to make this trip?"

"Yes, I can't move on with my job here until I know what happened to Amora. She can do ongoing damage even though her shapeshifting abilities are gone. Her witchcraft over people's minds is probably increasing." I said, zipping up my collapsible bag.

"Do me one thing. Take this book with you." Grandpa Pete said, handing me a copy of Jack Kerouac's *Big Sur.*"

"Why this book?"

"It will help when you think you're going out of your skin. Kerouac was a conflicted man, but in this book he writes about such peaceful solitude. It was like the elements of Big Sur spoke to him, kept his demons at bay."

I gently placed his gift in between my underwear and my favorite robe. I left Anderson with plenty of curiosity, plenty of stomach-churning anxiety. In a non-descript restaurant off the interstate in Nebraska, I opened Kerouac's book waiting for my steak entrée. His loose construction of no paragraphs and sentence structure surprisingly held my attention throughout my dinner and the overnight in the Nebraska plains.

Entering the interchange to San Jose, I got a text buzzing my phone laying in my console. I regretted not taking Luther's advice, having my phone hooked into a technology to my dashboard. Every two minutes a loud buzzing went off until I stopped at a combination gas station and mini-mart twelve miles from Carmel, California.

The text read from Luther: *"The real estate agency Thornton used is Carmel-By-The-Sea Realty in the central part of Carmel's business district."*

I walked into the real estate office. I was hit head on with an aura of wealth, making me feel underdressed and out classed. So, I decided to use my charm.

"Hello, this office makes me feel ashamed I did not dress to impress. Been on the road for days, living in the same pair of jeans. I'm here in this beautiful country to find my long lost uncle, Wesley Thornton. Did he ever use your services?" I inquired with the Super Model-essk receptionist.

"Let me get Mrs. Fenway. She was his agent."

A tall very attractive finely dressed woman approached. "Well, you're in for a treat. Mr. Thornton moved in to one of our most popular properties. Come back to my office, I will give you the directions."

Her office was roomy and flanked with striking contemporary artwork depicting the area's breathtaking scenery. "Sit down, dear. Go by this map with your focal point being Highway 1 which goes through the center of Big Sur Village." She said warmly.

"Could you help me with one more thing?" I asked, giving her my most sincere smile.

She nodded, flipping back her blonde streaked cascading hair. I found that gesture amusing. I had to fight back laughter when I asked, "In your opinion where is the most famous restaurant that defines Big Sur? I want to treat my uncle my first night I spend with him."

"It's Nepenthe Restaurant, 29 miles south of Carmel. I got to confess, it's pricy." She said, looking at me in a factious manner of superiority.

"Oh, I get it." I laughed. "These clothes are my travelling garb. With my recent promotion, I've plenty of funds. No worries there." I stood up, and politely shook her hand. I wanted to stand over her and give her a peace of my mind but I restrained myself.

After making accommodations in Carmel, I thought I better look the part of a substantial woman. I went into one of the trendy boutiques along the downtown strip leading down to the beach area. My initial plan entailed getting acquainted with the type of wealthy residents Wesley would find himself fraternizing with.

A simple-lined dress in perriwinkle blue draped over the curves of my body in a nice way suited my thinking of blending in. The sales consultant smiled wide and gasped. "Oh, my! With your classic brunette coloring, this dress is perfect for you!"

Thankful to my grandfather for slipping in ten one-hundred dollar bills into the Kerouac book. I was able to purchase the dress with no panic—then use what was left for the pricy Nepenthe. I knew full well my Indiana economic sense had to pulled up several notches to compete in this inflated environment.

South on Nacimiento Fergusson Road to Highway 1, I drove up a significant incline to the redwood contemporary structure of Nepenthe. Inside, it looked to me with a sizable crowd milling around. I had arrived at the mid-point of the cocktail hour. Most of the patrons were dressed casual, something I did not realize on my shopping errand earlier in the day. Instead of blending in, I stuck out. This caused me to feel very nervous and quite uneasy.

Even though I felt as if I was over dressed, I thought a drink would give me courage. I began casually walking around exploring with a glass of Pinot Grigio in my hand. I wanted a scotch and soda, but thought the wine seemed more appropriate.

I planted myself in front of a stone half-moon shaped fireplace structure overlooking a spectacular view of the San Lucias mountain range. To my back, I heard a man's voice. "I'm impressed. For once, a lady who knows how to look like a finely dressed female."

I turned around to see an attractive older man slender but well put together. He was dressed as though he got off the 18th hole at Pebble Beach. His eyes were aquamarine and when he smiled his teeth gleamed in the pre-dusk outdoor light.

"Thank you, I think. I was led to believe this restaurant required an upgrade in the dress code. I'm a novice to Big Sur etiquette, being from the Midwest." I answered back, thankful it didn't take long for someone to talk to me.

"I'm supposed to meet my new friend Wesley. He's from Indiana." The man said, still smiling.

"Wow! This is truly a small world. My uncle is Wesley Thornton, speaks with a slight Irish brough."

"That's the fella. Tell you what. Join me at one of those terrace tables over there and wait with me. He will be surprised to see you, I'm sure."

I was more than compliant, and inwardly delighted. We drank a carafe of more Pinot Grigio which the blue-eyed gentleman was insistent on buying. He took my hand, his eyes became more blue. We made conversation on the "getting-to-know-you" nature for the next twenty-five minutes.

He looked at his watch, then leaned in closer to my left shoulder. "Pretty lady in order for you to stick around. It looks like Wesley is not going to show. Have dinner with me."

"Only if we go halves on the check. I insist." I said, making the rules which might simmer him down on his obvious sexual expectations.

Halfway through dinner my newfound gentleman friend offered intriguing table talk. His eyes got real animated as he related to me the last time he joined Wesley for a few drinks at this place.

"There was a chill in the air with a huge storm bringing in crashing tides along with lots of cloud cover that night. Wesley and I hung out at the community fire wall. There came over a friend of my late wife. Wesley struck up an instant connection with her. They eventually left together." He said, then lowered his head. He seemed to exhibit a genuine concern of sorts.

"You seem to be upset about something." I asked, my observation radar was out in abundance.

He took a large sip from his wine glass. "Irene is also one of my oldest friends. Yesterday, I went into the art gallery that she owns. Her assistant told me she hadn't seen her in almost a week. She had called her home several times, leaving a message each time."

"Seems to be a mystery brewing, although I must tell you my uncle has a knack of snarling in a female. She could be with him for days, and not bother to go about her daily routine. She is probably caught up in his infectious Irish charm." I said, making up a convincing story.

He took my hand once again, this time kissing the top of my hand very softly. He leaned close, breathing distance. His breath gave off a faint odor of the soft Grigio. It seemed kissable enough if the pleasing inclination arose. "I must confess. You have the same ability as your uncle. Your charm has totally disarmed me. Can we pay the check and move on to my place?"

I found that most tempting. I was getting more attracted by the minute, or maybe the wine was overtaking me. I decided to come clean. "You're a nice man and I find you very attractive. So, you need to know. Back in Indiana, I'm a detective. Wesley Thornton had helped me with a difficult case. I still need his help. That's why I'm here."

He drew back, and lost his boyish smile. He jumped out of his seat, to throw down four twenty dollar bills. "Here's my share." He walked away, and did not look back. So much for my alluring charm, it disappeared by his quiet contempt for my obvious lie of being Wesley's niece.

Chapter Thirty-One
Dinner with Wesley

That night I tossed and turned. My mind restless, but fighting a deep exhaustion for fear I would experience images taking me into a dark realm I wanted no part of. After an early morning shower, I knew I had to face Wesley Thornton.

Finishing up lunch at one of the downtown Carmel's outdoor bistros, I called Luther. He bellowed almost seeming to be amused. "Well, I was wondering when you would make contact. Any sign of Thornton in your California search?"

"Yes, I got an address. First, I need to ask some questions about the disappearance of a local woman Wesley was seen with at an infamous gathering place in Big Sur."

"Are you thinking another victim of our escaped prisoner? Maybe, by some strange reason Wesley moved to the West coast because of some insane loyalty to Amora?"

I huffed, then answered. "You know from a sleepless night, I have a hunch his move had nothing to do with Amora."

"Hope you've got your handgun and badge on hand. In case you need them." Luther said.

"Oh, for sure. Didn't leave home without them. I'll contact back when the dust settles if it does. I've got such a dread rolling around in my head." I told him, then clicked off.

The waitress came over to give me the check. I asked her. "Do you happen to know an Irene who is a widow living in the Big Sur area?"

She nodded enthusiastically. "Oh, Yes! She's my older sister's employer. Irene owns and runs the art gallery down by the beach entrance at the end of this street."

I walked down the steep hill getting closer to the view of the crystal glimmering ocean waters lightly moving along the sun-bleached shore. I came to a storefront with a sign reading, "Ocean Front Gallery". The white walls were graced with large striking large paintings depicting ocean scenes in contemporary modular styles in bright bold colors.

A medium-height redhead dressed in a close-fitting green dress approached me, "Welcome to Ocean Front. How can I direct you today?"

"Well, I'm looking for Irene. Is she in today?" I told her, flashing my badge in case the young lady got cagey in wanting to talk to me.

The bouncy overly cheerful young woman changed into a somber person. She waved me to follow her away from the other patrons studying the artwork in the connecting rooms. "I haven't seen her for at least a week. I've called her home several times, and left messages. This isn't like her."

I pulled out my small notebook from my back pocket. "Could you give me an address? I can take a gander. See is I get any clues to help with this mystery. If I get any clues, I will get ahold of the nearest authorities here."

"Yes, by all means, officer. Her home is a couple of miles past the Big Sur Village on Highway 1, 3555 View Terra." She was most agreeable to give me the address.

I drove past the village after getting a tip from a clerk at a gas station and combination mini-mart. I looked for the sign called View Terra where the surrounding land became elevated. The clerk had told me the lengthy curvy stretch was one treacherous climb. My car ascended, then on the right I could feel a sudden drop. There were large evergreen trees on each side of a noticeable white paved entrance. The driveway curved going up some. I passed a three-car garage where there appeared numbers in fancy script, "3555".

I drove closer to a small neo-French estate in antique white stucco and light blue trim. I parked in front of the last garage door. I walked over to each window at each garage door. No cars to be found. I saw only a line of large garden tools along the back wall.

I knocked on the shiny brass front door. Getting no answer, I checked to see if the door was locked. The front door was securely locked. I walked through a natural fence of California blue pine to the back of the house. The long succession of glassed-in windows showed no one walking through the visible kitchen and adjoining living room.

In my mind, I imagined making my way through the natural illuminated series of rooms out into the redwood deck. I couldn't imagine how one person could live with such a vast space of living quarters when I had always been satisfied with my two bedroom walk-up apartment in Anderson.

After all, I was witness to all the trimmings of a wealthy billion-dollar community. Ironic in such amazing rich splendor, what I was soon to find out made my search all that more bizarre.

I walked around the house to the bottom of the deck steps. I turned around, viewing the sun-glistened moderate-moving waves, kissing ever so lightly onto the jutted-up dark-coned brown and purple rocks. Obviously the woman was nowhere to be found. Perhaps, driving to my final destination in this exclusive paradise she would be there under the captive company of my main focus. She was hopefully alive and well, mystery solved.

At the hour of the day brilliant colors gave a display of dusk, I came to the residence of Wesley Thornton. To my surprise, I spied the Rathbone black limousine parked along the curved driveway. *Well, well, he kept something to remind himself of his station in life before his vast wealth landed him among the rich and famous of Big Sur.*

I got to the front door. To my surprise it was opened only a few inches opened, but enough to give me access to the interior. I made my way through the spacious natural illuminated series of rooms decorated in a minimum of style, neutral colors with an occasional overstuffed sectional, then to my left a long glass table I assumed to be the dining area.

I walked outside through the open sliding-glass doors to a huge dark red planked deck made of redwood. I got to the railing, viewing the sun-glistened slow-moving waves kissing up against the jutted-up dark brown and purple cone-shaped rocks. I leaned over to realize the house was secured from several rafters over a canyon below.

My vision followed the sound of the waves to my far right. There sat a rock formation very large and domed. It seemed to be the exterior of a seaside cavern. In the center there was a weathered door. An odd presence in the midst of the waves and various sea caves making up the canyon.

A white-haired man opened the door, holding a towel. I squinted to get better focus as he came more into view carefully walking from rock to rock. It was Wesley dressed in a white water-stained T-shirt and a pair of tan shorts.

I stood fast as he made his way to the top step of the deck. Facing me, he spoke with no evidence of surprise. "I knew you would track me down. You've come just in time. I'm going to prepare dinner."

Before I answered back, I noticed under the towel was a plastic bag containing some kind of pale-pink mystery meat. "Wesley, you obviously making dinner for your guest. I know about Irene."

He brushed past me. "No Irene here. On the contrary, join me for dinner."

I was hoping for more words about the missing woman. He offered nothing to my usual curiosity. I chose not to push, in order to get what I had initially drove two thousand miles to find out. I dread that got me to this very site changed to a strong overpowering sense of danger.

I followed him to the open-air kitchen. Sitting down at the center bar, I could hear the soft movement of the nearby ocean waters gliding over the rock formations. Nothing of the blasting of wind and waves Kerouac would describe on his first initial meeting to his Big Sur experience at his friends small cabin under the Bixby Bridge.

"This place is truly spectacular. I might ruin your tranquil day with questions I've been mulling over since Amora escaped the Anderson jail."

"No worries. You wouldn't be true to form if you didn't follow through with your detective side." Wesley stated as he brought out, what was inside the bag. He held the slimy contents in his hands like he was holding a new born baby, rinsing the animal organs in the double sink.

"Tonight, I have a yen for sweetbreads. In the oven over there I have pork chops which you will probably prefer to eat than what I am holding here." He continued.

"What is it with you gourmets loving sweetbreads. I only got introduced to that once." I stopped, my mind went to the time I watched who I thought was Amado, consuming the pancreas of an animal in only a few bites. Suddenly, I felt a panic. My mind reeled in a question. *What in the hell is going on? Why do I panic seeing him prepare this?*

I gathered up my inward shakiness coupled with paralyzing terror to put on a performance of someone cooler minded. "So, you did expect me?"

"I got a message from one of my golfing buddies. He described you, then gave me a warning. You told him about being a cop. I'm sure he was taken off guard. He is known as the community playboy ever since his wife passed away."

Even through my present state of fear, I found that comment amusing. "Oh, Yeah! The guy who I had dinner with, looking like a Don Johnson clone. When I told him about being a cop, you should have seen his face. He bolted."

Tossing a salad, then Wesley juxtaposed movements to sear the sweetbreads. I decided to go for broke and ask an obvious question. "You know where Amora is. Don't you?"

"My dear detective, we will discuss your insatiable curiosity about Amora over our entrees. Be patient, you will get what you came for."

I sat there, watching his calculated synchronization of preparing the pinkish-pale animal organ. Odd, it reminded me of how Amado/Amora instructed the waiter months ago his personal specifics on how the sweetbreads were to be prepared. Panic gripped my heart like someone had magically entered my chest cavity to grab onto my beating organ. The same precise steps were being taken.

My plate looked like I was being served from a chef in the most elegant of restaurants—two large pork chops smothered in a mustard sauce complemented by a salad lightly tossed in a poppy seed dressing. I joined Wesley at the glass dining room table. I stared down at the head of the table to see he was only to eat the sweetbreads.

Enjoying the red wine served along with the delicious entrée, I had to probe. "Well, you promised to feed my insatiable desire to know about Amora."

He swallowed the last bite of the sweetbreads, then took a sip from his wine glass. "Let me begin by confessing a conviction I have possessed. Amora had always been somewhat of a troubling soul even before her manifestation. After her escape, she realized her invincibility with her powers to control others by the legendary dark magic of this phenomena of aswang. She had to be destroyed forever."

"How was that to be done?"

"Are you done eating?"

I wrinkled my nose, confused about the state of my meal consumption. "Why ask that?"

"My answer will not only repulse you, but will put you into instant fright." Wesley stated, his blue eyes brightened in extreme intensity.

"I have to know. Screw on how I will react!" I was to the point of no return.

"Before I divulge what went on, I need to make an important trip to the master bath. Don't go away."

I sat there, my mind racing as to his sudden trip to the bathroom. Another fact that set my mind to wonder—he took his half-full wine glass with him. Nothing to do but wait, so I poured more wine into my glass.

Chapter Thirty-Two

It Turned Strange

At the end of my wine glass, I got my desire. Wesley came close to where I was seated. He raised his wine glass to meet the sun's rays coming in from the slightly opened white sheer curtains of the series of sliding glass doors going out to the terrace. His back was to me. He drank down the remainder of the wine in one gulp.

He turned around to face me. "I don't have much time. I poisoned Amora. After your visit that day with Detective Charles, I cut up her lifeless body. I buried her various body parts deep in separate places around the Rathbone Estate. The next morning before the gardener showed up, I dug up every body part."

Wesley came close to me, so close we were eye to eye. My heart began to race, and my temples beat with sudden fear. He explained further, his blue eyes became almost black. "I proceeded to burn every part of her once beautiful head and body. Before her heart stopped, she bit my hand with a curse attached."

He could see I was about to speak. Holding out his hand to stop me. "One more thing to confess before my end. She cursed me to crave human organs for the rest of my days. If I tried to eat anything normal, my body would go into tremendous tremors of pain. Promise me, you will do your job as you are programmed to do. Take your investigative skills to examine my storage in the rock cavern down by the canyon where the rocks meet the ocean."

With that last request, he collapsed to the floor carpet. I jumped out of my seat to tend to him. His breathing was not evident. I ran into the kitchen to find some latex gloves.

Going back to Wesley, I took off his T-shirt, and put my head to his chest. I took his right wrist and felt for a pulse. There wasn't one. I checked the right side of his neck, nothing. My emotions I worked hard to keep in check. I got up and took his wine glass to smell the rim and the inside of the glass. There was a lingering odor of what was identified to me as battery fluid, very faint but it was there.

I called 911, then made my way to the canyon cavern he spoke of. Inside, I could feel right away the coolness, enough that I wanted to put on my jacket. I looked at each shelf of a tall metal shelving unit. From what I could see through thick plastic, there were what I thought to be animal internal organs.

My forward vision intent to discover, on the second to the last shelf at the bottom was what looked to be human feet. I jumped back. My breathing accelerated, full terror had took over. I stood there frozen. Wesley's words came back, "cursed to crave human organs". Those sweetbreads he prepared with my watchful eyes were human pancreas—my thinking, could be the pancreas of Irene, the local widow who left The Nepenthe with him.

I walked out onto the slimy rocks very carefully. My breathing seemed as if I would choke at any moment, leaving me to fall into the rocks and moving waves. The images I took in appalled me. As I took in cleansing breaths to slow down my inner hysterics. I realized Wesley did the humane act of ending his life. He appeared to me by our first meeting at the Rathbone front door to be a most distinguished gentleman with a trained air of knowing how to serve the aristocracy.

Taking in the natural movement of the ocean hitting the rocks, I could hear the slamming of car doors. I carefully moved away from the series of pointed rocks and landed my feet onto a small green hill. I raised up to my tiptoes, and saw two squad cars parked in the half-moon shaped driveway.

When I got to the inside of the house, I heard loud pounding coming from the front door. I opened the front door. One officer said. "You called of a possible suicide?"

"Yes, I did. I was having dinner with the victim when I witnessed him collapsing from something deadly in his wine glass. Come on in." I followed three officers making their way to Wesley's lifeless body.

I stood there while two uniformed officers walked around the victim, as the plain-clothed officer studied every orifice of the body. He got up and approached me. "I'm Detective Burley. Who are you?"

"I'm Detective Glenda McMahan from the APD Detective Division in Anderson, Indiana. Wesley knew some last minute details of an investigation I was part of. He did this to himself after he had made me dinner." I said, then presented Detective Burley with my badge.

Detective Burley scratched his tousled light brown hair. "Yeah, Anderson, don't tell me, you were part of that bizarre case of some wealthy beauty who manifested as a creature for a specific purpose to fulfill some phenomenon. In what country was that?"

"The curse originated in the Philippines. Let me be clear. Wesley Thornton was previously the butler to the Rathbone Dynasty of big Pharma in Indianapolis. He confessed to me of poisoning Amora who was attacker and the killer of all our twenty-eight victims. Before she died, she bit his hand to pass on a curse to him. There is proof of that curse down below in the canyon off of the terrace. I went in there." I told the detective, my rising hysteria growing with every word.

The detective did not say a word. He went over to where the wine glass sat on top of the dining table. He took out a small kit, dusting it for prints. Then dusted Wesley for any prints, making sure I wasn't lying. He smelled all around the glass.

"This glass inside and around the rim smells like battery fluid." He said, looking over at me. I chimed in. "Like you, getting some gloves, I came to same conclusion. Let me take you upstairs to the master bath."

The other officers followed us upstairs to the spacious bathroom. Detective Burley carefully went over every part of the sink, cabinets underneath and over the sink. He came to a bottle with only a few pills inside. He handed the pills to one of the officers. The other officer brought him a ceramic apothecary bowl where it was evident something had been mixed together.

Detective Burley smelled the white powder left in the bowl. He nodded his green eyes seemed fascinated. He handed me the bowl. "Take a whiff and tell me what you smell."

"That is the battery fluid smell. Before he confessed all to me, he took his wine glass up to the bathroom. Came down to where I was still seated and drank down the remains of what was in the glass."

"Looks to me, detective, so far you're kosher enough. Give me some kind of card so I can get back to you." He said.

I gave him my card. "Let me warn you what you and your men find in that cavern is as strange as what you had read about my case back in Indiana." I left him and his men to figure out the details from here. My emotions were kept in check. I left Detective Burley without a whimper.

There was no need to stick around. At this precise moment, I knew I was not in full control of my emotions. A gentleman, a vital part of a difficult case was responsible for seeing to it my partner and I did not see any prosecution.

I was a witness to his sad horrific state of affairs. I watched him destroy himself with no means to stop him. Wesley Thornton had morphed into an impossible middle between humanity and extreme savage.

From a tip at a local Big Sur Village gas up station, I drove to Pfeiffer Beach. From getting halfway through Kerouac's book, I took his lead to experience what Big Sur could do for me—especially in my present manic state of mind. I parked my car underneath a cleared area from a group of cypress trees.

I walked with no thought to how many miles I put under my sand-spattered tennis shoes. I took off my shoes when I came to a large rock formation out into the deeper waters of the ocean. The buff colored slanted rock possessed an opening about the size of a double-garage door.

One of the locals I talked to when I filled up my car with gas told me about "Neptune's Door". She said, it was along Pfeiffer Beach, and really something to see.

I walked into the slow-moving surf where there was shallow water. I stopped at a flat area of rock large enough for me to sit down. I rested with my feet as the aquamarine waters cooled my ankles. I looked down to see tiny fish swimming around my toes from the transparent water.

I broke down and cried, my tears drenching my face and neck. Anybody in earshot distance would have thought I was going through a nervous breakdown. My sobs were extremely loud and I let out a blood-curdling scream twice amongst the demonstration of sorrowful tears. I took the ankle-deep salt water and washed my face, then looked up at "Neptune's Door".

I stopped crying, and stood up. I took my badge out of my left back pocket and threw it as hard as could into the moving waters coming towards me. My eyes followed the shiny object giving way to the natural propelling velocity. I sighed a deep breath of one who had discarded a heavy weight of consciousness and sorrow.

Suddenly a strong noisy wind forced the deep blue waters to crash up onto the large rock formation. The foam on the tops of the incoming high waves beat against the rim of the door opening seemed like some ogresome castle dripping wet with the ocean's slaverous lips of foam.

I immediately moved back onto the damp nut brown shore. I screamed out in the direction of the waves hitting up against "Neptune's Door". I don't know why I did this. It could have happened due to the culmination of trauma I witnessed from Wesley's confession. His suicide mission, a pathetic way to get his soul back somehow almost made me physically ill.

I shouted out. "Amora, your memory is gone. You cannot torment me anymore!"

The waves noticeably died down. I could now see the blue sky appear from "Neptune's Door". For the first time since I arrived in California, I thought about Grandpa Pete. Which meant to me—time to get back to Indiana.

For the first time since I woke up in the Anderson city hospital, I didn't feel that nagging dread—churning and churning to such a magnitude I thought I would scream. My badge was gone, slowly going out with the rolling surf. My prospects were zero, but I knew I wasn't going mad anymore.

Chapter Thirty-Three

Indiana Bound, For Now

The long arduous drive through the Rocky Mountain states landed me in a small town found in a valley, Crested Butte, Colorado. I was so clouded by my trauma in Big Sur, I failed to map my way back to the Midwest via through the Southwestern states.

Crested Butte, a few hundred miles south of Denver had received a blanket of eight inches of snow from a passing storm. I was told by the local sheriff to lay low for a couple of days until the town could shovel its way clear. I was able to take in the local charm with visits to the art galleries and the town square.

Experiencing the daily activity of a provincial pleasant mountainous community, helped me feel more normal. I basked in the warmth and sweet flavor of a small town.

My lightweight jacket had lost its benefits of warmth when I had driven out of Central California. In a sporting goods store on the main street of Crested Butte, I was helped by a kind middle-aged clerk to purchase a warm quilted navy blue coat. The clerk and I struck up a friendly conversation.

She had originally come from Ft. Wayne, Indiana. When the passing of marijuana, medical and recreational became legal in Colorado, her family moved to Crested Butte. Her husband, a horticulturist bought a dispensary outside of Crested Butte while her twin sons attended Denver University.

I told her. "I'm on leave from a detective division in Central Indiana. I've been kicking around the idea of trying something else."

She didn't ask why, not to pry. She said in an enthusiastic tone. "You know, you ought to look into working for a security firm. This kind of service, especially now, pays very well. All the dispensaries in the state needs good people."

I was given a solid idea to my latest conundrum. It was definitely something to consider. This tempting aura of hope put me in a better mood. I ran into the sheriff on my way to the inn I was staying. He had given me the green light and directions on how to get back on the interstate going east back to Indiana.

I showed up at Grandpa Pete's front door two days later. I was bone tired and bleary-eyed from the long road back. Grace opened the door. "Praise be! You get in here, young lady!"

Behind Grace stood Lola, my favorite great dane. She gave me a "Hello" bark and brought up her right paw for me to shake. I got on my knees, throwing my arms around her large neck. Maybe due to the exhaustion of the drive or what I went through in Big Sur, I cried into Lola's short-haired reddish-brown smooth coat.

Grandpa Pete came into the foyer. Witnessing my emotional state, he stared at Grace with a confused expression. Grace scolded him. "Peter, all this girl needs is rest. Let's get her upstairs. I'm sure she's got bags to bring in." His cue to bring my little pittance of luggage into the house.

I refrained from any protests of not wanting any tender love care from the doting Grace. I basked in her heavy-handed mothering. Surprised that I actually liked it. I hit the warm bed like a brick and passed out for hours.

I woke up to Grace gently telling me to come downstairs for dinner. I raised up with one eye opened. "I'll be down after I wash my face. Thanks, Grace. I could use some of your food."

I doused my head in the sink filled up with cold water. The rustling movement of drying my hair from a nearby towel brought me into a sigh. I voiced to myself out loud. "Wow, that was the sleep of the dead. Sure glad to be home."

Walking down the steps, my nose got wind of Grace's food preparations in the direction of the formal dining room. I sat down to a presentation of roast beef, a large bowl of fluffy mashed potatoes, and a platter of steamed broccoli and cauliflower. I nodded to Grandpa Pete still looking at me as though I had come back from the dead while I filled up my plate.

After taking in a few delicious bites, I noticed a glimmering Christmas tree gracing the corner of the dining room close to the kitchen archway. I petted Lola as she draped her large paws over my feet. I said to my grandfather and Grace. "Well, it looks like I need to get into the Holiday spirit."

"Do you think you can after what you experienced in California? When you walked into the foyer, you looked like you had come back from some kind of a war." Grandpa Pete said, showing some indifference.

"Peter, maybe Glenda is glad to be back. She might not be ready to talk about what happened out west." Grace interjected.

I sat up straight, looking at them with my somber detective face. "No, you both deserve to know. The escaped prisoner Amora Rathbone had cursed the man I went to California to question."

I cut a dripping bite of roast beef doused it in Grace's brown gravy. I studied it, then said. "Amora had given Wesley a parting gift. He took his life because of the last act of witchcraft she laid on him from a lethal bite on his hand. It was a horror in every sense of the word." I put the fork in my mouth.

Grace and Grandpa Pete were speechless, and made no more discussion on my California trip. I spent the remainder of the evening helping Grace clear off the dining room table. We shared harmless small talk while I joined in on the kitchen clean-up. I was beginning to warm up to her. She held over me without saying anything—sense of normalcy, life does go on in spite of the worst of a plunge into the very heart of darkness.

For the coming days, I put on my new warm coat from my Colorado stay-over and took Lola with me on long walks throughout the Edgewood neighborhood. I stopped in front of Edgewood Golf Course clubhouse. Lola had a moment to relieve herself, while I admired the colonial type of Southern charm architecture the clubhouse possessed.

I bent down to scoop up the remains from Lola into a plastic Ziploc bag. Lola gave forth a threatening bark. I raised up to discover a woman bundled up in winter gear. She approached Lola and I with extreme caution.

"Easy girl, she's a friend." I spoke softly to Lola, who immediately stepped down from her sentry dog stance.

Wyla Stark got a safe distance in order not to provoke Lola. I said. "Well, well, you must have spoken to Luther. He's the only one who knew I was back."

"Yeah! He told me you were on leave for an undetermined period. I went to your apartment first. Your landlady was getting her mail. She said you might be staying with your grandfather. I guess, you're enjoying how the upper crust lives."

"Not really fraternize with the uppity neighbors. From what happened in California, I needed a touch of family." I told her.

"Got something really important to discuss. Can we go back to your grandfather's warm house? I'm not one for this frozen stuff."

"Sure, Lola is at ease. She won't eat you." I reassured Wyla who looked rather rattled as Lola moved closer to her.

We walked at a steady pace. Wyla would let out a heavy sigh and say with a whining tone. "Shit, here in Anderson, it's colder than Chicago!"

I took Wyla into the kitchen to make her some hot chocolate. I thought a hot treat would take her mind off on how frozen she felt. I laughed at her. "Sit down. I'll make you something sweet and hot. Boy, you sure showed a nervousness towards Lola!"

"She's as big as I horse. Dogs, not a fan of, I take to cats more." Wyla said, after taking off her hat, gloves and coat.

She sat down at the kitchen table in the center of the spacious kitchen. Her eyes were glued to the cinnamon rolls neatly piled onto a plate. "Hey, mind if I take one. Didn't catch any breakfast."

"Sure, help yourself." As I stirred the lowfat milk slowly until it got to almost boiling, I took out chocolate syrup from the pantry. I carefully poured some of the syrup as I turned off the burner.

I joined her after pouring the milky brown mixture into two mugs. I handed her a mug. "You're the last person I expected to visit me."

She swallowed another bite of roll, then washed it down with the hot chocolate. Wiped her fingers on a nearby napkin, she exhibited an expression of sheer delight. "Well, delicious morning snack by the way, but let me get real serious here. I've been preparing for Paris and thought it best to wait until I heard from the boys."

"Have you heard from them yet?"

"Oh, yeah, I got the green light two days ago. I told them I needed to see you before I booked a flight."

She sat there and finished consuming the roll. I was about to say something. She held up her hand after she had taken in more of the hot drink. "They stressed to make it quick. They have hooked up with a group of people who specialize in searching through the miles of tunnels underneath Paris."

I got suspicious on her deliberate stalling tactic. "Why come see me?"

"I know you found out something serious about Amora. Luther told me, you have been real vague about going back to work. Something gives with you!" Wyla stressed, she leaned in with a wild stare.

I raised up my mug, then wiped my mouth. "Wesley had taken care of Amora for good, a gory demise, cutting up her body parts, then burning her. She cursed him before she breathed her last. I sat there while he confessed. He took in the remainder of his wine, and in minutes he was dead."

Wyla got up paced around the table, then looked down on me. "There's something more. Things got stranger when you found Wesley, I know it!"

I nodded, staring into her dark eyes. "Wesley had been cursed to crave human organs and flesh from a bite she gave him. He wasn't Aswang, but something he couldn't live with. Before he died, he told me to investigate a large rock formation that he used as a storage for human remains. It was so sinister, and so haunting to see those contents in heavy plastic. I lost it for a bit, and threw my badge into the ocean."

Wyla let out a yelp, so loud I thought Grace would run in any minute, wanting to know what happened. She backed up and pointed at me, "This is so perfect! You have to come to Paris with me. What other lame idea of a job do you have?"

"I got an idea of working security in one of those dispensaries in Colorado. They pay big. The country there is unbelievable." I said. Wyla saw through my lame rationalization.

"Not for you, No! Maybe some time when you've reached retirement age. Glenda, think about it! You crossed into the supernatural through this case. It got even stranger, when you went out west. If you go out to Colorado, you'll lose your bloody mind." Wyla stressed.

I thought about the long journey into darkness—the intense fear, not able to think of me making it through another year. I thought about in the middle of all this terror and chaos—I possessed an energy of such magnitude in the very thick of the worse scenario. In intense pain but the exhilaration of capturing that creature, seeing it change back into a human, and the prize of taking Amora to jail precluded all the experienced horror.

I reacted to Wyla in a practical way. "I need to get a passport. Can you wait for that?"

Wyla clapped her hands together. "I knew I could get you to go! Don't have a worry about the passport. I can speed things up a bit."

"Only one question remains. Has it been determined, an aswang is what we would be after?"

"Well, let me answer you this. Paul and John have talked to the leading magistrate on the Ile de la Cite where two victims were found. Their gruesome remains were among the area aftermath of the Notre Dame De Paris affected by that fire. The very same remains from our infamous case here in Indiana." Wyla said, sitting back down.

"You're in the general direction. Now, I have to go. I have to see the remains of those victims." I said, realizing Wyla knew exactly how to trigger my insatiable curiosity. That idea of a security post became a passing consideration. Those who I love and those who I have worked with for so many years I knew in my heart and mind, will see this development as purely reckless and downright lunacy.

Chapter Thirty-Four
Saying Farewell

Until the day I was to leave with Wyla, I wrestled greatly before retiring for the night with the rationality of my decision. *What if I got stranded in this international city, not knowing a lick of French? Could this adventure back into the supernatural be defined as a foolish dead end?*

As I waited for my passport, I tried to streamline through language lessons from Rosetta Stone at the city's public library. Going back and forth after each session, I would drive past the APD building. A well of tears would build up, shaking my head vigorously. I wished I could go back in time. Seeing myself flatly refuse Mitch Gable's insistence on taking that first interview with Melanie Rossen. I laughed to myself, realizing no one could refuse Gable on anything. He had always been a force to contend with, but to me in retrospect—he was my greatest teacher, no matter how caustic.

What transpired could not be wished away. The journey into evil tainted my comfort zone for law enforcement. Wyla was right that morning in the hospital. I would not be able to live a normal life. All the affinities most folks hope to be a part of. It would not manifest for me. Besides, when she laid out the familiar type of case defined after the fire of the historic cathedral—my nagging curiosity could not be ignored.

Grandpa Pete yelled for me, interrupting my umpteenth mind over matter wrestling match. I came down to the foyer, meeting his glaring puzzled expression.

"What's this?" He asked, holding up an official unopened white envelope.

This was the moment I dreaded. To tell my grandfather I was leaving for Paris. "Well, that should be my passport. I wasn't going to say anything until it arrived." I told him as he handed it to me.

He stood over me, as I opened it. I was right. There it was. The trip was official now. I showed him the passport. "That's what your visit with that FBI agent was about. Where are you going this time?"

I cowered my head, holding onto the passport like it was a security blanket. I met his angry stare. "Grandpa Pete, we are going to Paris. There is a possibility an aswang has murdered two victims among the burned rubble of the Notre Dame cathedral."

"I knew it deep in my gut. She had talked you into something dreadful!"

"Wyla's partners, John, George and Paul are there now making arrangements for us to join those who are experts searching around in the tunnels of the Paris Underground." I told him, refusing to look into his angry face.

"Glenda, are you aware any activity in those tunnels is illegal? If you and your group are caught, you'll go to jail!" He yelled.

"If in our search we find this abomination to be the guilty one. We can stop another cursed one to kill, one victim after another. I have to do my part!" I said, defending myself.

There was no reasoning with my grandfather. He stormed away from my presence. The proof of why I dreaded a confrontation with him was confirmed in all its unpleasantness. At that moment, I alerted Wyla from the house phone to the passport arrival.

She demonstrated her usual non-committal dryness. "I'll be there to pick you up tonight. I'll book us a redeye flight out of Indianapolis

International. You can pay me back later. Be ready to roll by 8 p.m., don't want no lingering goodbyes from your family."

I sent Luther a text. *"Wyla and I will be at Unc's a little after 8 p.m. tonight. Meet us. It's important!"* A lump formed in my throat. I hated goodbyes. I had not been good where saying farewell meant emotional displays. Luther and I were not ones for any shared sentiment during our years of being partners. I had to see him before we flew off on a journey of such uncertainty and danger.

It didn't take too long until I got a reply from Luther. He answered back in a text, *"I'll be there. What you didn't say gives me a sneaking suspicion I won't like what you are up to with Agent Stark."*

Grace came into my bedroom. "Glenda, your grandfather is in a mood. Can you tell me what's going on with him?"

I zipped up my large wheeled bag. I took her hand. "Grace, he's upset due to my sudden trip to Paris. The situation there could lead to another brush with the supernatural."

Her wide-eyed stare and expression coming from her pursed lips showed some understanding. "That explains it."

"I'm done packing. Let's go downstairs and I'll help you make dinner." I said, giving her a rare demonstration of warmth her way.

When Wyla arrived, I tried to say goodbye to Grandpa Pete. He avoided the gesture by skirting passed me to pound on his grand piano, the classic theme of *"Gone With The Wind".* I waved farewell in Grace's direction. I could not linger. She had tears in her eyes. Wyla took my large bag while I put my shoulder bag around my left shoulder and chest. I followed her outside with my overnight bag in my right hand.

We packed away my things in the backseat next to Wyla's bags. I got into the passenger seat, then turned to her as she turned on the car. "When is our flight?"

"We don't have to check in until 10:30 PM."

"Luther is meeting us at Unc's White Corner downtown. I wanted to make sure he knows what's up with this trip."

Wyla gave me an annoyed look. "I hope there won't be any cornball emotional shit going on!"

I shook my head. "You've seen the way Luther and I act around each other. He deserves to be read the specifics of what we are going after."

Wyla shrugged her shoulders and followed through on my request. As we walked up to the bar, Unc raised up his large long fingers. "Well, bloody Hell, Peter told me you two would be coming in. His voice sounded real somber. Whose this official-looking lass?"

"This is my travel partner and one of the FBI agents who worked with Luther and I, Wyla Stark." I said, as Wyla and I took a center seat at the long bar.

"First, before I demand an explanation of this trip. What do you ladies want?"

Wyla ordered first. "I'm driving. Have you any fresh coffee brewing?"

"That I do. Glenda, my beauty, are you in for a frosted draft?"

I nodded an affirmative response. I turned to hear a door slam, and discovered Luther approaching the bar. Unc asked him. "Detective, what can I get you?"

"I have a feeling, I'll need a double scotch. Unc, put it in a short glass on the rocks." Luther told him, glaring at Wyla.

Luther proceeded to point to a booth as Unc went to tend to our orders. "Let's go over to the dining room."

We made our positions at the four-man booth next to the series of windows along the Main Street side of the establishment. Wyla and I faced our stern-eyed, one-man interrogator. I observed. "Luther, you seem to be bracing up for bad news."

"You too are on the search for another aswang. Am I right?"

Wyla answered. "How astute of you. John, Paul, and George are waiting for us in Paris. They will probably have some update tidbits when we get there."

Unc brought us our drinks. He put his small round metal tray on a table next to us. He sat down beside Luther. "I need to hear the details."

Luther took a sip of his drink, turned to Unc. "So do I."

"Wyla, you give them what they want." I said.

"The aftermath of the fire of the Notre Dame de Paris was full of a large clean-up crew along with law enforcement. Two city workers found a torn up gentleman with certain body parts missing. As the workers got the attention of some officials, they found a woman's body with the same gruesome remains among the buried rubble from the fallen spire." Wyla explained, sipping on her coffee.

Unc stopped her with his long hairy arm. "Wait! Could the broken up remains be the result of the metal structure falling from such a high distance?"

"The guys got access to one of the leading magistrates giving them some details of the autopsies. The internal organs vacated showed jagged edges on surrounding tissues coming from an razor-sharp teeth and definite claw marks. Last week they tracked down the city's cataphiles who were able to give them more facts linking to this legend."Wyla said.

Luther interjected, "I read an article recently about these cataphiles. Those individuals getting access to the underground tunnels through opening up of man holes in the city streets."

"Is this information you gave me the only facts you have?" Unc asked.

"Well, it's enough for Glenda and I to see for ourselves." Wyla said, then turned to me.

I followed her lead. "The last thing I want to do is get intertwined into another supernatural series of murders. What began five months ago, I can't turn back to normal detective cases. There could be another aswang performing heinous acts of continuing evil. They don't stop!" I answered with a special emphasis on—they don't stop.

Unc turned around to discover four couples walking to two tables on the other side of the dining room. "Duty calls. If possible you brave ladies come back to us in one piece!"

Luther took the last gulp from his short glass. He pulled out his iPhone. Looking at the lighted screen, "oops! I've got a text from Althea."

Wyla and I took that as a cue to follow him out to his Escalade. I felt uncomfortable about how to act out a proper goodbye. He unlocked the driver's side. Wyla and I stood a few yards away from where he was.

I asked him. "Do you know the sex yet?"

He opened the door, and hiked his lanky long leg onto the floorboard of the front seat. He yelled out. "It's a girl! Althea wants to name her Glenda."

That did it! He made it emotional. The sobbing overwhelmed me. It rose from my throat, producing a waterfall coming down from my eyes to my cheeks and onto my chin. Wyla silently and quickly got me into the car.

On the road to the Indianapolis International Airport, Wyla decided to let me weep. I grieved over the tension between Grandpa Pete and I. I knew I would miss my unique give-and-take relationship from Luther Charles.

As Wyla and I waited in line to check in our bags, I knew I couldn't go back even if I wanted to. Boarding the plane and listening to the surrounding passengers in our coach section, I told myself—this would be the last time I would harbor regret on my new lot in life. I was defined to be a formidable searcher to find and fight against the greatest of evil.

Lightning Source UK Ltd.
Milton Keynes UK
UKHW010636020821
388172UK00001B/63